Sugar and Spice

The DL Diaries, Book One

Shondra Jackson

www.chancespress.com

Sugar and Spice: The DL Diaries, Book One

Copyright © 2014 by Shondra Jackson

For Miss Gerrie,
For reasons well known to you!

Acknowledgments

Thanks to Candy Holiday for all of the invaluable information on the ATL and sharing her love of the fine brothers out there.

Chapter One

Marcus reached down under the covers and started to stroke his veiny, beefy cock while his wife, Rochelle, lightly snored next to him. She always did what many thought was the traditional male thing by falling asleep right after sex. Not him. How could he possibly sleep after willing his body to do so many things that felt alien to him? Caressing her breasts, grabbing her ass, penetrating her with his pulsating dick. She'd never guess the things he had to think of just to get him through these husbandly duties at least once a week. And it was getting harder and harder with each year they were married. He knew many men would love to fuck his wife. With her loose wild chestnut brown curls, full bosom, and ample ass, she'd been a former beauty queen. Miss Black Georgia, Miss Teen Georgia, Miss something else he couldn't remember which was a surprise since she talked about her pageant days like she was still eighteen versus a thirty year old.

He carefully slid out from under the covers and tiptoed over discarded clothes to reach the bathroom. He quietly shut the door and flipped on the light. He looked at his tall, six foot two, muscular frame and ran his hands over that six pack he worked so hard to achieve. His skin was a smooth light cocoa brown due to his part Native American ancestry and his eyes were a dark brown almost black. He kept his curly black hair to a short half-inch.

"You are one big fucking black stud," Rochelle had said on their second date when she slid her hands down the front of his pants and gripped his impressive, even when soft, manhood.

They met when both were seniors in college and married soon after graduation with what can only be called a swift, whirlwind courtship.

He knew then he didn't feel what he should for her. Now, after eight years of marriage it was practically torture to climb into bed with her and feign sexual interest. He had to keep up the ruse though because no one...and he meant no one...could ever find out his truth. If they did, gone would be the upper level corporate management job he held at his father-in-law's chain of upscale coffee cafes, Sugar and Spice, the number one coffee chain in Atlanta and the rest of the Deep South. If people knew what made his cock hard and his balls swell with cum, he'd lose his marriage and the social standing that went with being married to Harold McNair's daughter, the former belle of upper crust African-American crust Georgia. He had worked too hard scraping his way up from a lower middle class family in rural Georgia to let this all slip away. But as time went on, even though he was in great physical health, he couldn't overcome this foreboding feeling that he was slowly dying emotionally and spiritually...losing himself with each passing year.

He turned the shower on almost scalding hot to wash away the sex sweat and stepped inside. He gripped his now stiffened cock and thought of what he knew would get him off. He thought about grabbing him...Eric...from behind. Bending him over and pulling down those tight slacks he wore to work to expose his pale bubble butt. He thought about how he loved to spit in the palm of his hand and then rub his spit over this white boy's tight little butt hole. Then he'd take out a rubber because you could never be too careful, and then he'd ram his cock into that warm inviting little manpussy. Eric would do his usual moaning and screaming out what a stud Marcus was and how no other man could compare. Marcus would pound hard into him and call Eric his little pussy bitch. He'd make him whimper and tell him how good his big black cock felt in his little white hole. Marcus would fuck him hard and Eric, the perfect bottom boy, knew how to take it long and so deep that Marcus wouldn't have been surprised if his cum had shot out of Eric's mouth. Marcus would reach under and grab Eric's much smaller but rock hard penis and stroke it as he fucked him.

Suddenly, Marcus shot his cum all on the wall of the shower, and he tried to catch his breath.

Finally.

Release.

If he thought about Eric with herculean force and effort he could get hard enough to penetrate his wife and at least look like he was going through the motions.

He could sense that Rochelle felt the unspoken disconnect though, and she was gradually turning bitter and hard to handle. Things had been made even worse by him and Rochelle moving into his in-law's while their house went through a remodel. Marcus couldn't believe he let himself get talked into that one.

He could feel his in-law's eyes on him every night at dinner. Harold, uptight and conservative in a dress shirt and tie, always looked like the Atlanta's Top African-American Businessman of the Year 2008 he was. Harold's wife, Imelda, who was half-black and half-Filipina, was still a fiery exotic looking beauty at fifty-three years old with her shoulder length black hair and almond shaped eyes. Imelda was always prim and proper and done up in dress and make up no matter what day or time it happened to be.

He knew that his in-laws were getting frustrated. Where were the grandchildren that would one day take over the caffeine dynasty they had worked so hard to create? Rochelle was their only child and all the pressure was on their daughter to produce an heir.

Marcus kept finding excuses not to have children. He wanted to wait until he turned thirty. He wanted to work his way up to management and prove himself to his father-in-law first. He wanted to get the house remodeling done. He had simply started to run out of excuses, and he knew it.

He wiped the cum off the shower wall, turned off the water, and began to dry himself off. Maybe now he'd finally get some sleep.

When he opened the medicine cabinet to take out the deodorant he noticed Rochelle's birth control pill container. He opened it up, and his suspicions proved correct once again. There were way too many pills left. He'd been tracking it for weeks. Rochelle thought she had outsmarted him. She'd plead ignorance or an accident once she got knocked up, and then he'd be trapped. Little did she know he had her beat by a mile. He practically deserved an Academy Award for faking an orgasm during sex, something he knew many wives had learned to do for their husbands. With him and his wife, the roles were reversed. He never came inside her. In fact, he never even got wet with precum when he was with her...not like he did with Eric when a puddle of salty jizz would practically form in his underwear.

Rochelle wouldn't get pregnant anytime soon if he had anything to do with it. But how much longer could he keep this going before he felt totally and completely empty inside?

With that thought in his head, he walked back into the bedroom, got under the covers, and willed himself to a deep dark sleep to a state where none of his secrets threatened the life he had built.

Rochelle woke up, stretched, and wiped the sleep from her eyes. The bright morning sun shone through the bedroom window and warmed her face. When she sat up she noticed that the alarm clock read nine-thirty. For years, she'd gotten up the same time as Marcus since she felt she should see him off every morning before work. When she gradually had to admit to herself that he didn't seem to care she stopped. But then Marcus didn't seem to care about a lot of things anymore including her body, and things only got worse when they moved into her parents. Temporarily staying in the house that she grew up in seemed like a good idea at the time, but she'd quickly grown to regret it with her mother constantly haranguing her about grandchildren.

"You don't do anything with your days," her mother, Imelda, had said just yesterday as the two of them ate a light lunch of a Caesar salad by the pool. "All you do is shop. A woman needs more than that. And you're not getting any younger when it comes to having children."

Rochelle had sighed loudly and hoped her mother would take the hint that this topic was off-limits but no.

"Are you planning on wasting your days until you can't conceive anymore?"

"Marcus wants us to wait a little longer," Rochelle had said, repeating the same information she'd told her mother more times than she could count.

"Marcus, Marcus, Marcus," Imelda repeated. "He may be good at business, but the man needs his family duties to be prioritized."

The truth was that Rochelle would love to start a family, and she'd even grown so desperate as to conveniently "forget" to take her birth control pills. But then he never came inside her when they had sex, and he had been stupid enough to believe that she hadn't realized it. This, of course, made her wonder where he *did* get off.

She threw back the covers and grabbed the red silk robe that was draped over the antique chair next to the bed. Slipping the robe on, she enjoyed the way the soft fabric tickled her smooth skin giving her more of a rush than sex with Marcus had done in a very long time.

While looking at herself in the bedroom mirror, a wave of sadness went through her body. Why did her husband appear to be so checked out when it came to the marriage? She was still just as beautiful as the day she married him if she did say so herself. Her weekly visits with a trainer, a masseuse, spa visits, and weekly hair appointments were the closest things she had in her life when it came to "work." But Marcus didn't look the least bit interested anymore.

She found herself second guessing her femininity and sexuality. Other men noticed her so why not her husband? When they first married the sex had been wild and often. Although, even back then she sensed that Marcus was distant during sex, and she couldn't quite put her finger on why. Each year just progressed to worse and worse.

Divorce? Not an option.

She was Rochelle McNair DuBois, and she'd never failed at anything before. No one in her family had ever been divorced. She'd be damned that she'd be the first. But her frustration with a passionless marriage and a husband that always looked more interested in financial spreadsheets had begun to wear her down. She had become snappier, more sensitive, and just fucking frustrated.

"Please be sure to double-check the drain," she heard her mother say downstairs and outside.

She walked over to her window and peeked through the curtains.

Him.

Her mother was talking to the man who cleaned the pool and occasionally worked in the gardens of their fashionable home in the Bucktown district of Atlanta. And what a man he was. The first time Rochelle saw him a few weeks back when she and Marcus moved in she'd practically had her breath taken away by beauty.

She pulled the curtains apart just a few centimeters more for a better look.

Damn.

The man was just as hot as always. Walking sex. That's how she'd describe him.

Her mother was pointing something out to him next to the pool house.

She didn't even know his name for the longest, but it had been him she thought of when Marcus penetrated her. It was the only way she had gotten any pleasure from it. When she heard her mother call him

Tyrone it became that name she thought of over and over in her mind as her husband entered her.

God.

She could lick him all over.

He wore a tight white t-shirt which accentuated his strong, worked out, tattooed biceps. His jeans hung low around his waist and threatened to fall down exposing his cock and balls as she had a feeling he wore no underwear.

His skin was a light tawny color, and his eyes hinted at perhaps some Asian background mixed with some strong, hunky black man-god. It all gave him an aura of exoticness that immensely added to his striking good looks.

Suddenly, Rochelle felt a stirring deep inside she didn't often feel these days.

Today would be just the perfect day for some sunbathing.

"I want those reports by noon, ladies and gentleman. Noon means noon. Not 12:15 and not twelve-thirty. Thank you," Harold McNair said to his marketing staff as the meeting wound down.

Harold's employees got up and scrambled off to make his command come true...everyone except Marcus that is. He wanted to lay the groundwork for a long lunch to take care of some of his *needs*. Even though he sometimes felt like his father-in-law had him by the balls, Marcus made it a point not to jump as fast as everyone else did. But Marcus also knew that the only true way he'd get his Harold off his back would be to produce an heir something he knew he'd need to produce sooner and probably not later.

It took everything Marcus had not to groan. His father-in-law was a grueling task master, but Marcus had to give it to him that that was probably the key to his success. Harold took no bullshit from anyone, and that included Marcus. Marcus knew he never would have climbed the corporate ranks so quickly without being Harold McNair's son-in-law, and Harold never missed a chance to reiterate this point.

"When can I expect the first round of marketing proposals for the new sandwich line?"

"The ad agency will be here tomorrow morning with sample items," Marcus answered, even though he had already mentioned this in the previous meeting.

"Good. I expect to be wowed," Harold said, reaching for his coffee and taking a long slurp.

"I'm meeting with a new commercial real estate agent this afternoon about the new Garden Hills location, so it may be later in the day before I'm back."

Marcus sucked in a breath and waited to see if Harold would challenge or question him. Instead Harold just took off his glasses and wiped them down with a tissue.

"How's the remodel coming?" Harold asked him and changing the topic much to Marcus's pleasure.

"Getting tired of having us around, Harold?"

"Of course not. Family is *everything*."

Before Harold could bring up possible grandchildren for the millionth time, Marcus got up and gathered his paperwork.

"I'll let you know how the meeting this afternoon goes."

Heading down the hallway towards his office, Marcus saw Eric, Harold's second assistant, slightly bent over and picking up a box that UPS had just delivered.

Damn.

The boy had an ass on him...the kind of juicy butt that was just begging for a hung guy to slam into it and make the little boy bitch moan and beg for a good dicking. There was just something about how this cute little white guy would be submissive to him that made his heavy cock fill with pulsating blood and harden.

Besides an out-of-this-world ass, Eric had blond hair, sky blue eyes, and smooth skin. He wasn't overly muscular but tight and toned in the right places which was what Marcus preferred. Marcus liked to fuck a guy who was smaller than him and would yield to his control. Marcus enjoyed seeing his throbbing ebony cock sliding between Eric's creamy white butt cheeks. The contrast in skin color turned him on even more...somehow in his mind this added to the tabooness of the situation.

"Eric," Marcus called out in his deep voice.

Eric picked up the box and set in on his desk before turning around and meeting Marcus's gaze.

"Let my assistant know I'll be out at meetings most of the afternoon," Marcus said.

Eric's eyes lit up.

Their code words.

"Of course, Mr. DuBois," Eric answered, turning quickly away so as not to raise suspicion amongst the other employees working in the office.

Marcus continued walking down the hall with an extra spark in his step just at the thought of what would happen this afternoon.

Eric, who would now take his lunch break, would meet Marcus in just mere minutes after he took a short taxi ride to the St. Regis Hotel on West Paces Ferry Road. Marcus would have already paid for the room with a prepaid American Express card, and he'd be waiting for Eric there...wearing nothing but a smile and a rock-hard penis.

"I hope you don't mind me out here while you work," Rochelle said, appearing at the edge of the pool while Tyrone fished some leaves out of the pool.

She loved the way his eyes widened as he looked up and saw her wearing her favorite baby pink bikini. The thought that she had turned him on was enough to send waves of heat rushing through her body. She *wanted* him to *want* her.

"Of course not, Ms. DuBois. I'll be done here in just a few minutes," Tyrone said, flashing her a pearly white smile.

She wondered to herself why he didn't do something else such as modeling. God knew he'd be a natural. He was just too damned handsome not to do something that capitalized on his amazing looks.

"Take your time," she answered, while casually and slowly draping her towel on one of the pool chaise lounge to give him a good view of her front *and* back.

When she turned back around she caught him staring. He quickly looked away, and Rochelle felt positively thrilled.

She lay down on the lounge and put on her sunglasses the better to stare at Tyrone without him realizing it. She loved the idea of toying with him and leaving him guessing if she was watching him as much as she guessed he wanted to look at her.

When Eric walked into the hotel room at the St. Regis, he felt the butterflies in his stomach going into overdrive as they always did when he met Marcus. He'd never experienced the mind-blowing hard pounding kind of sex that Marcus gave him with any other man. He didn't know if it was because of Marcus's hefty dick which had proved to be almost overwhelming when it came to penetration or if it was the taboo factor of it all…being fucked by a man married to the boss' daughter. Or perhaps it was a combo of it all. What Eric did know was that his own cock hardened and dripped wet with precum just at the thought of Marcus's brawny body.

If his friends knew...

Eric would never tell his buddies about his hot and heavy affair with the married stud from the office. What would they think of the guy who spent weekends volunteering at the local gay and lesbian center and helping organize the city's gay pride every year fucking a closeted man? Eric didn't know how he had ended up being a cliché. He never intended for this to happen. He tried to date and meet compatible men, but every time one tried to get too close Eric would start shutting down. As hard as it was to admit to himself, one of the things he liked about Marcus was that he *did* go home to his wife and left Eric's perfectly guarded heart alone. Well mostly. Eric knew his feelings for Marcus were becoming much more complicated. He yearned to have Marcus wrap those sinewy arms around him after sex.

"Sup?" Marcus said sitting on the bed naked, his legs spread, his thick shaft hard, pulsating and waiting to be serviced.

Eric's heart began to thunder in his chest.

"Hey," Eric said, shutting the door behind him.

He walked towards Marcus with desire threatening to explode from every cell in his body.

"On your knees and suck it," Marcus ordered.

Cross, uncross her legs. Rochelle DuBois repeated the movement every few minutes, and he began to think she was cock teasing him. She *wanted* him to look.

Tyrone silently cleaned the pool, scooping out leaves and small sticks and trying not to think about his dick hardening in his low riding jeans.

What did she want with him?

Shit. He knew she at least wanted him to look at her. Out of the corner of his eye, he'd caught her staring at him from the window. *Lusting.* She wanted to be noticed and to feel as if she were being desired. He wondered if her husband didn't do enough to make her feel attractive. It certainly wasn't the first time a married woman flirted with him on the job. Bored housewives. Pool guy. Not that much of a stretch. But, he never ever went there. There was too much pocket money to lose if things went bad, and he needed every dime to pay for his acting classes and savings to move to Los Angeles.

He knew women like Rochelle DuBois only thought of him as a walking piece of wood, someone to service them and make them feel like the seductress they so wanted to be. But there was a fucking lot more to Tyrone Benjamin Baxter. He had dreams of acting, landing on the big movie screen, and getting the hell out of Atlanta where he'd spent his entire life growing up being raised by his grandmother after his cracked out mom disappeared. His mother may have turned out to be nothing, but he'd make it. He do it for himself and for his grandmother.

"Are you from Atlanta?" Rochelle DuBois asked out of nowhere as he finished up.

"Born and raised," he answered.

She took off her sunshades. He knew it was to remove any doubt that she was looking at him, studying him, wondering what was in his pants.

"Would you mind?" she asked, holding up a bottle of sunscreen. "My back."

He knew that this would be entering dangerous territory. She was testing him. If it had been any other place any other time, he wouldn't hesitate. He'd give her what she wanted, and he'd enjoy giving it to her, too. With a rack like hers, he'd love to go inside her and make her scream in ecstasy.

He'd suck the nipples on those titties until she became all wet and wanting more. But here? Not worth it. But he knew there was only one correct answer to her question.

He could tell that she knew he was hesitating as she cocked an eyebrow. He had to answer and quick. As much as he hated it, his job probably depended on it. Maybe all she wanted was some slight flirtation and that would take care of it.

"Sure. No prob," Tyrone said, walking to the other side of the pool.

He sat in the chaise lounge next to her, and she turned around exposing her back to him.

Just do it quick and move on to taking care of the garden, he thought to himself.

He squirted some of the creamy lotion in his hands and began to rub it into her back. He could feel Rochelle pressing her back into his hands increasing the friction and the heat of his touch.

Out of the corner of his eye, he saw Imelda DuBois staring at them from the kitchen window.

Shit.

"That's right. Suck it, bitch!" Marcus said, pressing Eric's head down and his cock deeper down the white boy's throat.

Eric gagged for a second, but then started expertly deep throating it. The guy was an expert cocksucker. He knew how to engulf Marcus's dick in a way no one else, man or woman, ever had.

"You like that, don't you, white boy?" Marcus demanded, slightly pulling on Eric's blonde locks.

Eric groaned in pleasure.

Suddenly, Marcus forced Eric's head up and made him look him in the eye.

"Stand up, pull down you pants, and bend over," Marcus said in a soft but gruff voice.

On command, Eric did what Marcus asked him and exposed his high and tight ass to him. Marcus stood up and teased Eric's little pucker hole with the head of his dick.

He glanced at the clock next to the bed and noticed that he would need to be back at work soon.

Fuck.

The office. He hated that place. He hated being under his father-in-law's watch. But here with Eric, he was totally in control. He ran the entire show, and he fucking loved it.

He spread those sweet little ass cheeks of Eric and got ready to give the little twink the fuck of his lifetime.

Chapter Two

"Dinner will be ready in twenty minutes, Ms. McNair," Thelma, the family's long-suffering maid, said as she placed Imelda McNair's evening glass of Merlot next to her in the family study.

Imelda gave a barely perceptible nod and continued glaring at her daughter while Rochelle flipped through the latest issue of Vogue.

Thelma, sensing when to do so, made a quick exit and headed back to check on the cook in the kitchen.

"Are you going to say anything, Mother? Or are you just going to continue to stare at me?" Rochelle asked, flipping the pages.

"Is this really what you do all day? Lying in the sun? Reading magazines? Going shopping?"

Rochelle dropped her magazine and met her mother's stare.

"Why don't you just say what you really mean? Ever since Marcus and I moved in you've been giving me judgmental looks and loud sighs. I really think staying here during the remodel may have been a mistake."

"Rochelle, your father and I didn't sacrifice and struggle throughout our youth to build a business empire and to send you to the best schools so you could just waste away your days married to a man…" Imelda said, her voice trailing off. She shrugged her shoulders and patted her perfectly coiffed up do. She may have been in her fifties, but Imelda prided herself on her smooth light brown skin and still naturally dark hair.

"If I remember correctly, father was the one who built the business," Rochelle said, hoping to deliver a sting.

"Oh, really? You think that was all your father's doing? I was the one who balanced the bills, kept food on the table, and volunteered at all the right places so your father could make the connections he needed to make. You've had everything given to you to the point that you really have no idea, do you? And now..."

Rochelle stood up, put a hand on her hip, and glared at her mother. "And now what?"

"You're not getting younger, Rochelle," Imelda said, standing, too.

"Meaning?"

"When are you Marcus starting a family? Your father and I have both been patiently waiting."

"I don't think that's any of your business," Rochelle said, exasperated.

"Don't you *ever* speak to me in that tone again!" Imelda yelled, before giving her daughter a stinging slap across the face.

Stunned, Rochelle stood there motionless, the anger rising from her gut. Her mother *always* got what she wanted, and it wasn't the first time she'd used the back of her hand to make her point.

"I've been watching you."

"What does that mean?" Rochelle demanded. "Watching me?"

"Yes, *watching you*. Your marriage is hanging on by a thread. I suggest you do something to pull it together, Rochelle. Even a blind man could see the distance between you and your husband. Our family doesn't do divorce," Imelda said. She took a deep breath, composing herself as if nothing has just happened. "I'll see you at dinner. Be sure to think about what I've said."

And with that, she left a shaking Rochelle behind.

As much as she hated to admit it, her mother was right about one thing. Her marriage was way off track, and her husband may be there in body but sure as hell not in mind. And finally, she was going to find out exactly why.

"End scene!" Roger, the acting teacher called out.

The class broke out into applause, and Tyrone felt elated. He had done what he believed his best scene in acting class so far, a scene from "Picnic" by William Inge.

"Good job, mister," Allison his scene partner said with a flirty smile, as she seductively ran a finger over his bicep.

"Thanks," he replied, before heading back to his seat with the other actors in the class.

As cute as she was with her auburn hair and green eyes, Tyrone did not want to go there. She'd been flirting with him from the moment they met in class. Tyrone had decided to keep his acting class free and clear of any future possible dating drama. He only wanted to focus on the craft he had only in the past year decided to completely go after…full force. There weren't a lot of acting classes in Atlanta, but with the cities burgeoning film and television industry, there were more opportunities than ever before. But it still wasn't the mecca for an actor, Los Angeles.

"That's it for tonight, everyone. I'll see you next week. Please get together with your scene partners to practice in the meantime," Roger announced.

As everyone started gathering their materials, Roger motioned at Tyrone to come over.

"What's up?" Tyrone asked.

"I wanted to share some information I found out with you," Roger said, pushing up his Buddy Holley black rimmed glasses. With his bushy gray beard, he had an easy going grandfather aura about him. "There are some open auditions tomorrow I think you should go for."

"Really?" Tyrone said, feeling the excitement build inside him. "Auditions for what?"

"The new Nate Jenkins film that will be shooting here in Atlanta. He's looking for local undiscovered talent to highlight in the film."

"Holy shit!" Tyrone said, unable to conceal his excitement.

Nate Jenkins was the hot-shot African-American film director who financed his first film, *She's Wat Sup,* a romantic comedy featuring upper-class black characters in Atlanta, by working full-time as a taxi driver. He shopped the film around to different festivals until it was picked up by a small distributor which in turn got the film onto screens first in Atlanta and then, eventually, the whole country. The film industry was taken aback when the low budget film managed to take in twenty million at the box office with its fresh take on contemporary black romance. From there, he signed a three picture deal and had churned out hit after hit and filmed all of the movies in Atlanta.

"I think you're good, Tyrone. Real good. And I rarely, and I mean *rarely*, say that. I think you should go for it."

A wave of uncertainty went through Tyrone's mind. As much as he wanted to be an actor and as much as people told him he could be a model, that little voice of doubt from the little boy whose mother left crept up in his mind.

"Do you really think so, Roger?"

"I do. Go. Give it a shot. You've got nothing to lose," Roger replied, handing him a piece of paper with the time and address.

Rochelle heard the shower in their bathroom running when she walked into their bedroom. Marcus's business clothes were haphazardly thrown on the bed.

Once again, he'd come home, snuck by her somehow, and headed straight to the shower before she could even talk to him. As much as it burned her up to admit it, her mother was right. Her marriage was totally off track. It had been so for so long she didn't even know what to do to get it back on track.

She sighed loudly and picked the clothes off the bed. Why couldn't he at least dump them in the closet?

That's when she smelled it. The shirt had some sort of men's cologne lingering on it but not any that Marcus owned. In fact, Marcus hated wearing cologne. So what...

"Hey," Marcus said, opening the door and walking out with a towel hung loosely around his waist.

"I thought you were going to be late for dinner *again*," she said not bothering to hide her displeasure.

"Well, I'm not. I'm here," he said, dropping his towel and letting her gaze at what she had but didn't have.

His cock and balls hung low and impressive. Why didn't he feel passion for her to use that tool like a man should on his wife?

"Did you get an update on the remodel?"

"May I remind you that it was your idea we stay here?" Marcus replied tersely.

He walked into the closet and began to dig for more casual clothes for dinner.

"No, you don't need to remind me, Marcus," she said, looking back at the shirt with the odd cologne smell.

She felt a new determination to get back in control of her marriage, her life, and have some fun.

"What do you think of his dick?"

"It's impressive," Eric said to his friend Curtis as they watched one of the dancers twirling his cock like a helicopter blade.

The two sat at a table at an all-male strip bar in Atlanta called Swinging Cox while sipping gin and tonics. Whenever he felt down, Eric could count on Curtis meeting him up for a drink and suggesting something wild for the evening. He only wished he could tell Curtis exactly why he was feeling down, but the shame he felt for being involved with a guy on the down low kept him from being honest. How could he tell his best friend, with the long-term boyfriend, that he was having an affair with a married man from his office? As supportive as Curtis was, he knew he would get a lecture.

What was he thinking?

Didn't he know he was just on a path to heartache?

Was he even thinking of the wife and what this may be doing to her?

How could he tell Curtis that when Marcus put his cock inside him it made him feel complete in a way that no other man had before? How could he tell him that it was the very fact that he was married and had a wife that he found so titillating? What did this say about him?

"Just impressive? You think the guy is just impressive? I mean look at that cock," Curtis said, chugging his cocktail.

"Aren't you practically married?" Eric asked jokingly.

"Doesn't matter where I get my appetite as long as I come home for dinner, right?" Curtis said, jabbing him in the side.

Eric laughed.

He looked back up at the stripper. He was beautiful. Shaggy, surfer light brown hair, a six pack, and low-hangers. But there was no way he could compete with the massive tool between Marcus's legs. The first time Marcus fucked him, he thought he might break him into half. The pain was so intense that Eric thought he might lose his mind. But then the pain switched to pleasure, and Marcus's cock filled him so totally and completely to the point that he thought he might be sent straight to heaven. Looking into Marcus's dark brown eyes as he lay on top of him and his dick pounding into him, Eric thought he might be transported straight to pleasure heaven. He wanted Marcus even deeper inside him if that were possible. But what really blew Eric away was when Marcus's fucking made him cum without even touching his dick. No top had ever done that to him.

Marcus's dick was like crack, and Eric's hole was the pipe to smoke it in.

How could he ever go back to "regular" sex? But the problem was that deep down he wanted more than sex with Marcus. But that could never be a possibility. Could it?

Chapter Three

The neighborhood looked like something straight out of a zombie movie: graffiti covered dilapidated buildings, empty eyed heroin addicts stumbling along the street in search of their next hit, and an utter sense of lawlessness. To say that Rochelle was a bit out of place was the understatement of the year. Yet, here she was parking her car next to a broken parking meter early on a Tuesday morning. The Bluff area of Atlanta had been notorious for years as a place you did not visit unless you absolutely needed to do so, and Rochelle had never dreamed that the need would arise for her.

She put on large, dark wraparound shades and exited the car looking like a scared cat ready to jump out of its skin and quickly walked towards a bar called, The Last Drop. The place looked like the sort of establishment one might visit to set up a hit on someone.

The strange scent that lingered on Marcus's clothes proved to be the last straw. She *had* to know what her husband was up to during those long hours he supposedly spent at work. Before bed the previous night, she snuck down to the study and called the one person she could count on to keep her lips shut tight, her friend Catherine, from her college sorority. The two of them became fast friends all those years ago, and they held each other's secrets tightly. Rochelle had held Catherine's hand while she waited for her turn in the abortion clinic after getting knocked up by the quarterback of their college football team, the same guy who told her to fuck off. Her pregnancy wasn't his problem. And Catherine had been the one to smash an empty Jagermeister bottle on top of Rochelle's date's head when he wouldn't take no for an answer.

Despite all of the years that had passed and that they were both married to successful, upper crust men, the two of them continued to have each other's backs. So, when Rochelle called her to get a referral on a private investigator, Catherine had a number at the ready. Rochelle didn't tell her exactly why she wanted to hire one, but Catherine was no fool. The fact that she had the number almost on the tip of her tongue spoke volumes.

"You don't want to meet him at his office in Midtown or anywhere remotely where you might run into somebody. At the very least, you want to meet him at a place if you were to be recognized that the other person wouldn't dare want to reveal they had been the same place.

The PI, a guy named Dan Wells, who sounded like he smoked a carton of cigarettes a day, had answered the phone late that night. He suggested The Last Drop in East Point without her even needing to mention that she needed to be super discreet.

When Rochelle reached the door of the bar, she wished she had one of those antibacterial wipes to open it with. She saw the hours of business posted next to the door. Every day. Six am to 2 am. Why anyone would be at this nasty bar at six in the morning was beyond her.

She walked in and looked around. The only people she saw at first were the bartender who looked like he had never gone home after the previous closing at two in the morning and a woman who nursed a beer and had greasy gray hair and an assortment of plastic shopping bags.

Rochelle anxiously began to wonder if she had come to the wrong place, but then she heard fingers snapping towards the back. That's when she saw the PI, a man who looked to be in his fifties with salt and pepper hair and the look of eating too many donuts, sitting at a booth by himself while smoking and drinking a shot of something. She hurried over and slid into the opposite side of the booth.

The PI cracked a smile and said sarcastically, "Nice sunshades. They don't draw attention in the least."

Rochelle self-consciously took off her shades and crammed them into her purse. Like she would know what to wear to a place like this!

She looked down at the designer sweat suit she wore and realized how it too made her stick out like a two bit prostitute in a five star Las Vegas hotel.

"Catherine said you're one the best," she said, cutting straight to business. She didn't want to spend one single second longer here than she needed to do so.

"Not one of the best...*the best*," the PI said, before chugging down what was left of his shot. "Breakfast of champions!"

Rochelle curled her lip in disgust. She couldn't believe it had all come to this. Her marriage had reached this point of complete and utter disaster.

"I want to know what my husband is up to during the day *and* the evening."

The PI studied her for a moment, and his gaze unnerved her.

"Look," he started to say, "You look like a nice lady. So, I'm going to be upfront with you."

"About?" Rochelle said, growing impatient. She just wanted to get on with it.

"I get a lot of wives that come to me wanting to know what their husbands are up to when they're out of sight. Thing is that when a lot of them find out I can tell they wished they never did. You know what they say about ignorance being bliss."

"I've never been into ignorance, Mr. Wells. I *want* to know exactly what my husband is doing and when. Don't hold back on me."

"Well," the PI said, stubbing out his cigarette in a chipped gray ashtray. "If that's what you want, that's what you'll get. But don't say I didn't warn you. You got the retainer?"

She reached into her jacket pocket and slid an envelope stuffed with cash across the table.

"That should more than cover it," Rochelle said, tapping her manicured nail against the table.

The PI took a quick look inside the envelope and then stuffed it into his pocket.

"I'll start today," he said.

"Good. I expect an update as soon as possible."

And with that, she got up and strode out of that rat hole of a bar hoping she'd never have to see the inside of it again.

Marcus made it a point to stop into a couple of the local Sugar and Spice locations during the week. He never announced who he was to the staff and instead just acted like a regular customer. He found the information he gained from these undercover trips to be invaluable. They gave him a sense of what new items, such as the baked goods, customers were interested in and if they bought them after looking at them. He also got first hand insight into the level of customer service. A customer service overhaul with a new training for managers had been one of the first things he'd done when his father-in-law had hired him to help run the rapidly growing chain. He knew how other people in the office saw him…just the boss' son-in-law. Success by nepotism. It drove him fucking nuts. He worked his ass off. In fact, he felt he had to work even extra hard to prove himself because of the family connection.

"What can I get you, sir?" the cashier asked when he made it to the front of the line finally. Five minutes. Way too long for people on their way to work in the morning.

"Large latte with skim milk," he said, noticing the barista in the corner whipping up the drinks.

The guy might be slow, but he was an A+ piece of ass. He looked to be college aged, with dark hair, and light eyes. He had the lean build of a runner or someone who just had a great metabolism due to his age. The black uniform pants he wore outlined and accentuated a tiny perky ass which was just the kind Marcus loved to fuck long and determinedly hard and rough.

He felt his phone vibrate in his pocket signaling a text message.

New files came in. I put them on your desk.

Eric. It was their code text for I want you to fuck me later today. Marcus felt his cock start to grow heavy as it swelled in his pants just at the thought. Part of him wished he could keep a guy like Eric in his bed so he could fuck him over and over whenever he felt like it versus straining towards the edge of the bed and away from his wife.

The burden of his double-life had started to weigh heavy. To make matters worse, he had a sense of impending disaster, but he didn't know why.

As soon as he sent the text, Eric felt desperate.

Why did this man have control over him? Why couldn't he find a regular well-adjusted out gay man to date?

Instead, he sat at his office desk at work and felt downright *used*. Yet he allowed it to happen over and over again. He felt doomed when it came to love and romance, but he just couldn't make that break from Marcus. He also had what he knew were pathetic fantasies that Marcus would leave his wife and pledge his everlasting love to him. Like the guy would do that when his father-in-law was his boss.

"Eric?"

He snapped back to the present and saw Shannon, one of the other assistants, standing next to his cubicle.

"You okay? You looked miles away," she commented.

"Yeah. I'm good. Just not enough coffee this morning."

"Well, there's donuts in the break room in you want one."

Normally, Eric would have shied away from the fried, sugary treats not wanting to put on weight for Marcus. *Fuck, Marcus.* What had he done for him lately outside of mind blowing sex? He was getting to the point where he needed...felt like he deserved...more.

"Donuts sound good," he said, getting up and heading to the break room.

"Tyrone Daniels? You're up," the young, energetic casting assistant said, sticking her head out the door into the waiting room.

When Tyrone arrived that morning his heart sunk when he saw at least fifty other men there for the same reason. The rest of the actors just looked more polished, more professional than he was. He knew he didn't stand a chance, but he figured that since he was there might as well see it to the end. That was the kind of man his grandmother had raised him to be, and he didn't want to let her down.

He practically jumped out of the chair and followed the assistant into the next room. Immediately, he noticed Nate Jenkins sitting behind a table with one man sitting on each side of him. They all had very serious looks on their faces. To his right, a guy stood behind a mounted camera and a bright light shone onto a spot about ten feet in front of Nate Jenkins.

"Into the light please," the guy on Jenkins' right said to Tyrone when he walked in.

Tyrone did as he was told. He felt beads of sweat forming on his forehead, and he tried in vain to will the perspiration to stop.

The guy on Jenkins' left said, "When I say action look straight into the camera and deliver your lines."

Nate Jenkins said nothing, but Tyrone keenly felt his eyes focused on him. Jenkins looked smaller in person than he did on the TV interviews Tyrone had seen. Jenkins was casually dressed in a black hoodie, jeans, and Vans sneakers, but he also gave out an air of confidence of being in charge all without saying a word.

"Action!" the guy on the left said.

Tyrone began the lines he had spent the past hour trying to memorize.

"Baby, you know you're the only one for me. You're all I think about. You're all that I *want*. Stay here tonight. Don't go."

Tyrone tried to inflect a sense of longing without turning into desperation and losing his manhood in the process.

"Thank you. We'll be in touch if you move on to the next step," the guy on the right said to him, before dismissing him by looking back down at his paperwork.

Tyrone's gaze met Nate Jenkins' one, and for some odd reason Jenkins' look gave him the idea he might actually get called back.

Rochelle thanked the gods that her mother was gone on a two day trip with some women from her old college sorority. Since her father and Marcus spent most of their time at the office...or at least that's what they said...it was the perfect opportunity for her to get to know Tyrone, the pool guy, just a little better. She knew it was his day to come back, and if Marcus was playing around, as she suspected, why shouldn't she? At least once. Before she provided Marcus with proof of his behavior, she might as well get her turn.

She picked out a neon green string bikini from her closet. Just touching the soft cloth gave her chills when combined with the thought of Tyrone touching the sensitive material, running his fingers underneath the string, and ultimately removing the bikini to ravage her naked body.

Rochelle sensed his attraction the day she had him put the lotion on her back. She could practically feel the heat coming off his erect cock. She knew he had been erect. How could he not be?

And with that thought, she changed into the bathing suit, grabbed the sun lotion, and headed downstairs.

Just as Tyrone pulled up to the McNair house in his Ford pick-up, his phone vibrated in his pocket. He was still a bundle of nerves after the audition and figured it was his grandmother checking on him. He had called her the night before asking her to say a prayer.

When he pulled out the phone though, he didn't recognize the number. Usually, he let those calls go to voicemail, but something told him to answer.

"Hello?"

"Tyrone Daniels?"

"Yes?"

"This is Nate Jenkins."

Tyrone felt like his heart stopped beneath his white tank top.

"Tyrone, are you there?" Nate Jenkins asked.

"Yes, I am," Tyrone answered, snapping himself out of the shock.

"We liked your audition this morning, and I wanted to invite you to a screen test tomorrow at noon. Same place you were today. Can you make it?"

"Of…of course," Tyrone stammered, his head spinning.

"Great. I look forward to seeing your, Tyrone. *Really* look forward to it. Bye."

Tyrone sat in his truck for a moment taking it all in. *Nate Jenkins.* The guy wanted to see him for a screen test for an actual film.

Holy.

Shit.

Tyrone jumped out of his truck and spun around.

"Hell, yes!" he screamed out to the world.

12:30 in the afternoon.

Dan Wells notated the time in his pocket notebook. That's when Marcus DuBois entered the hotel approximately ten minutes after a young white guy from the same office building went into the same building.

Wearing a business suit to blend in and pretending to talk on his cellphone, Dan entered the building. He'd sit in the lobby, pretend to be a guest, and type on his laptop as if he had important business to attend to at that moment all the while waiting for Marcus DuBois to come back down. Then he would shot some discreet photos. It didn't take Sherlock Holmes to guess why a businessman would visit a hotel in the middle of the day. The real story would be if the other guy came back down at the same time, which Dan already had a strong feeling would be the case.

He sighed loudly. After seeing marriage after marriage torn apart by infidelity, stealing, and drug use was it any wonder he couldn't picture himself getting married? That fact drove his mother bat shit crazy as the woman was yearning for grandkids. He supposed he could give her the grandkid without getting married, but that would still be messy with a woman involved.

Plus, he had to work tons of extra hours and take on additional cases because he had issues with both pussy and poker. He loved banging woman after woman he found via his phone app, Get a Piece Now. On the app, he met fellow nymphomaniacs such as himself that were all for banging without baggage. But even more than a nice piece of ass, Dan loved the high he got from playing big stakes poker at secret lounges in the Atlanta area with the occasional trip to Vegas. He rarely won much, but it was just the thought of the possibility that got him excited to the point of getting a hard-on with a winning hand.

So, that left him running after cheating wives and husbands day in day out and waiting for Marcus DuBois to unknowingly reveal his secret life.

When Marcus walked into the hotel room, he found Eric lying naked, face down on the bed with his legs spread. Next to his right foot was a bottle of lube and a wrapped condom.

Marcus's dick immediately stood at attention. He loved it when Eric offered up his ass in some of the most submissive ways possible. It made him feel more like "the man" in the situation and somehow helped him justify in his mind that he really wasn't gay. After all, he was the one doing the fucking.

Eric turned his head towards him, and Marcus shut the door.

"You ready for some big black cock in that tight little white boy hole?" Marcus asked in a demanding, harsh voice as he walked towards the bed, unbuckling his belt.

"Please, sir," Eric whimpered. "I need your huge real man cock inside me to feel complete."

Marcus unzipped his pants and let them fall to the floor, and he stepped out of them. He started to undo his tie and unbutton his shirt.

"How bad do you want it?" Marcus demanded.

"More than you can imagine," Eric said, seductively spreading his legs and ass cheeks further apart. "Please fuck me like you fuck your wife."

"I'll do more than that," Marcus said in a husky voice. "I'm going to fuck your brains out, you little pussy bitch."

Rochelle wondered if it was the thought of her pussy that put that big smile on Tyrone's face today. She lounged by the pool and pretended to read the latest popular novel, something about a vampire and an insipid teenage girl. But she could care less about what lay between the pages of the book. What she wanted was Tyrone laying his pipe inside her in the way that her husband never did.

When he arrived, Tyrone looked practically over the moon with his beaming smile, but she didn't know why. She sure as hell hoped it had to do with her.

"My mother is gone for the *whole day*. She said to be sure to tell you that she'll pay you for two weeks on Monday."

"Not a problem," Tyrone said, gathering the pool cleaner. Truth was he didn't care much at all right now about the McNair swimming pool. His mind was on that audition. *His big chance.* The break he'd be yearning for what felt like his whole life.

"It's nice to have the whole house to myself," Rochelle commented, trying to put out the bait.

But it backfired when Tyrone looked up at her from his work and said, "Oh, I'm sorry. Would you rather I do this tomorrow?"

"No!" she said a little too urgently. "I just mean it's nice not to have my mother around for a bit. As big as this house is, it sure can feel crowded. My husband and I are just staying here until our house is remodeled."

Tyrone just smiled and continued mixing pool cleaners.

Rochelle didn't know if they were on the same page or not. He was proving hard to read.

"Do you live far from here?" she asked, setting the book down on a small table next to the chaise lounge.

He looked back up at her this time with a curious look in his eye.

"Not far," he said.

She couldn't take it anymore! She spent way too much time in her life waiting, waiting, *waiting* for others to make the first move. Whether it was her parents telling her where to go to college and when she should have babies to practically having to throw herself at Marcus, she was sick of it all.

"Tyrone, can you be discreet when it comes to your workplace?"

"Discreet?" he asked, cocking an eyebrow.

"Yes. Discreet."

"Well, I consider myself a professional. I don't talk about my clients and their lives to anyone."

"Great!" she purred. "Because I want you to fuck me."

"Excuse me?" Tyrone said, his eyes growing wide.

"Fuck me, Tyrone. I can take one look at you and tell that you know exactly what it takes to make a woman feel good, and I know how to make *you* feel good. We're the only people here the whole day. I've had my eye on you the whole time."

"You have?" he asked. He had noticed her checking him out, but he would have never dreamed that she would be this bold. Sure, she was beautiful. But would it be worth it in the long run? He'd been hit on by lonely housewife clients before, but most of them didn't look like Rochelle DuBois. But still.

"Yes, I have, Tyrone," Rochelle said, slowly standing up to give him a good view of the goods that were being placed before him. "And I want you."

"Are you sure this is a…" Tyrone started to say. He couldn't believe he was considering this, but with the high he was on with his audition…why the hell not? She sure as hell was hot, and he hadn't been laid in what felt like forever he'd been so busy.

"I'm going to walk into the pool house, and I hope to have you follow me inside."

She slowly, confidently, and deliberately strode towards the pool house and walked inside leaving Tyrone to make a decision…and fast.

First, Dan saw Marcus DuBois exit the elevator first about forty-five minutes after he had gone up. The man looked slightly rumpled, and he watched Marcus try to smooth down his clothes as he quickly walked through the lobby and out to the valet.

About another ten minutes, the young white guy exited the elevator. His hair looked slightly wet as if he had just gotten out of the shower. Dan watched him quickly head towards the self-parking garage.

Well, that was that. Marcus DuBois was screwing a guy from his office. Wait until the uppity wife gets a hold of this information, Dan thought. She's going to roast his balls for a midday snack.

But Dan wouldn't tell her just yet. He needed more billable hours and a little more proof. He'd get more pictures to prove without a doubt. He was sure of that.

Dan packed up his laptop where he had been reading poker tips online and got up to leave. He paused when he remembered the other clients he had to work for that afternoon. He would definitely need more caffeine. So, he headed to the Sugar and Spice Café located in the lobby of the hotel.

"What took you so long?" Rochelle purred, even though it had only taken about a minute and a half for Tyrone to follow her inside the pool house.

She had already removed her top, exposing her quarter sized dark brown nipples…the ones she loved to have sucked on hard and rough.

"You sure about this?" Tyrone said, his eyes were focused on her tits.

Her tits. *Her pride and weapons of man destruction*!

"Are we going to talk all day? Or are we going to fuck, Tyrone?" she said, the adrenaline coursing through her veins as she became bolder by the moment.

Tyrone rushed towards her and pushed her down on the daybed in the pool house. He pressed the weight of his worked-out body on her and immediately took her left nipple into his mouth, sucking eagerly, hungrily.

"That's right, baby. Suck it," she cooed, running her hands over his strong back muscles.

She felt herself getting wet like she hadn't been in years. She would give him the animalistic fuck of his entire life.

She felt his hard-on pushing against the fabric of his jeans, and she could tell just what a monster he had below. She wanted every single centimeter shoved in her and pounding her like his life depended on it.

His hands roughly felt over her body as he continued to greedily sick her nipple. Eventually, his fingers made their way to the delicate fabric that separated her wet pussy from him.

"Rochelle!" a shrill voice called out.

"Shit!" Rochelle muttered, pushing Tyrone off of her. "It's my mother! Quick! Hide in the closet!"

Practically stumbling, Tyrone made a dash for closet where he hid himself.

Rochelle, quicker than she thought humanly possible, put her top back on.

Damnit! What the fuck?

"What are you doing in here?" Imelda asked, suddenly appearing in the doorway.

"I had to use the bathroom and didn't feel like going back in the house," she answered, barely containing the irritation in her voice.

"What are *you* doing here? Aren't you supposed to be in Savannah or something?"

"I got a migraine before we even left. So, I came back home. I'll be upstairs," she said, turning around, but then pausing for a moment. She whirled around and looked at her daughter again. "Where's Tyrone? The pool guy? His truck is outside."

"I don't know, mother. Maybe you passed him on your way in without noticing."

"Hmmm," was all Imelda grunted. She didn't look completely satisfied with her daughter's answer. "I'm going to probably be resting the whole afternoon to get rid of this headache. Be useful and answer the phone when it rings."

And with that, Imelda headed back to the house.

After a few moments, she said, "You can come out now."

The closet door opened, and Marcus walked back out. Now, he had beads of sweat on his forehead.

"She's gone now. She won't be back," Rochelle said, reaching behind to undo her top again.

"Wait!" Tyrone exclaimed.

"What?" Rachelle asked, the confusion all over her face.

"Look. You're beautiful and everything. I'd love to have sex with you I'm sure. But...I just don't think it's a good idea. I need this job too much, and I don't want to jeopardize it."

"But you won't..." Rochelle started to say.

"I'm sorry. I just can't," Tyrone said, quickly making his way to the door, walking out, and shutting the door behind him.

Rochelle stood frozen for a moment. She had been so close to *finally* getting sexually satisfied, and then her damn mother showed up.

Then, a voice that she tried to bury deep inside her when she thought of her sexual relationship with her husband crept out. If he had really wanted you, he would have stayed. He would have fucked you despite the risk and enjoyed it. But he didn't. Just like her husband displayed almost no desire for her, Tyrone had rejected her, too.

Men had always been rejecting her. Even though she was constantly told how beautiful she was, it didn't make a difference. There was something about her…something wrong…that drove men away.

And with that thought repeating over and over in her head, she picked up a crystal vase and threw it against the wall shattering it into hundreds of tiny pieces.

Chapter Four

His heart pounded in his chest. He felt a little dizzy. He tried to will himself not to sweat. Tyrone couldn't believe that he was actually about to have a callback with Nate Jenkins, right now the hottest African-American filmmaker in the industry.

As he sat in the lobby of Nate Jenkins' company, Upside Down Productions, he watched as a couple of other guys were called in to audition before him. Again, all the other guys auditioning looked smoother, more polished, and it left Tyrone wondering if he could really compete. He'd spent a couple of hours that morning trying to decide what to wear something he usually didn't put much thought into. He had finally settled on a fitted black t-shirt and jeans. Nothing fancy but something that hopefully showed off the time he dedicated to the gym.

You have to calm down, he thought. Confidence. Portray confidence!

The same casting assistant from the previous audition opened a door, poked her head out, and called, "Tyrone Daniels?"

"Yes," Tyrone said standing up and smoothing down his t-shirt.

The assistant let her eyes wander and take in all of him. She looked pleased as she smiled and said, "You're up, honey."

Tyrone took a deep breath and walked towards what he hoped was the next step in his future.

"I can't believe I get to see you twice in a week. You're usually so busy. Or at least you *say*," Curtis said to Eric as they both looked over the menu at a Mexican restaurant close to Eric's office.

"I *am* usually busy during the week, but today was slow. Can't I invite my best friend out to lunch?"

"Oh, I'll never turn down a free lunch," Curtis said with a chuckle. He ran a hand through his ginger reddish brown hair and his hazel eyes focused on Eric intently. "When are you going to tell me what's going on? What's wrong?"

"What do you mean?" Eric said, sitting down his menu.

Curtis had an unnerving ability to see right through him sometimes. They'd known each other since they both moved to Atlanta after college and ended up living in the same rat trap of a cheap apartment building. They'd been there to see each other through many of life's challenges, and Eric told him everything. Well. Almost everything.

The truth was that Eric had seen Marcus leave with a few of his peers at the office for lunch. Their almost daily fuck session wouldn't be happening today. And as much as Eric despised himself for being a slave to this man's penis, he just couldn't help himself. And to make matters worse he didn't know what to do about it. He had thought seriously of confiding in Curtis, but his own shame at the situation had kept him from doing so.

"You've seemed off for a few months now. You always look like your mind is preoccupied with something."

"It's just been a crazy time for me at work," Eric answered, trying to appear nonchalant.

"Um hmmm," Curtis mumbled.

The waiter came over, and they both ordered chicken tostada salads hold the sour cream and cheese and pretty much anything else that would taste good.

Curtis sighed loudly and leaned forward across the table.

"You know I love you, and I'd never judge you, right?" he asked Eric.

"Of course. Why do you say that?"

"Promise me you're not going to get mad when I say this," Curtis said, fiddling nervously with his napkin.

"What?" Eric asked. He could feel his defenses rising. What was it that Curtis *thought* he knew?

"You're sleeping with that good looking black guy that passed us in the hallway, aren't you?" Curtis asked, silencing Eric into shock. "And I bet he's married, isn't he?"

"I don't know what you're talking about!' Eric exclaimed feeling his face flush with warmth.

"Sweetie, it's okay. You can talk to me," Curtis said, in a soothing tone.

"I don't know…"

"I saw the way you looked at him, and I saw that quick but definite look he gave you as we were leaving your office to come here. You're sleeping with him, aren't you?"

"Christ," Eric groaned.

How did Curtis always manage to see *everything?*

"I'm not judging you, but…"

"But what?" Eric replied, practically admitting it.

"I'm just worried about you."

"It's nothing. Just a fling," Eric said, waving a hand dismissively. "It's just sex."

"I don't want you to get hurt. Guys on the down low will…"

"Will what? What do you know about it? Like I said, it's *just sex.*"

"I know because I've been there in the same exact position."

"What?" Eric replied shocked.

"Remember that first year we were here in Atlanta, and I was working for that advertising firm as an intern?"

"Yes."

"And remember how I suddenly had to go home to my parents in Alabama for a couple of weeks, and you thought something was going on?"

Eric thought back and began to vaguely remember.

"Yeah. You seemed depressed. I thought maybe you were homesick."

"I was heartbroken," Curtis said softly. "I had been having an affair with a married guy at work. A guy that looked a lot like the one from your office in fact. Handsome. Successful. Cocoa brown skin. Curly black hair. He was about ten years older than me. Had a wife. Two kids. He seduced me one night when we were alone in the office. Well, I let him seduce me. I wanted it. I thought he was one of the studliest guys I had ever seen in my life. We started sneaking out at lunch. Sometimes I…"

Curtis' voice trailed off, and Eric still tried to compose himself. He couldn't believe this story. He had known nothing of it before.

"Sometimes what?" Eric said.

"I'd blow him in his car with the tinted windows in our parking garage. I was sooo…well, naïve. Most people would have put two and two together and gotten four, but somehow I managed to get three. I got it in my head that this guy was going to leave his wife for me, and we'd move away to some small town in Vermont and open up a gay bed and breakfast or some shit like that."

"How did it end?"

"He simply told me that it was over, and if I valued my job, I would never mention it to anyone. He said he could tell I was getting too *close*, and he told me flat out he'd never leave his wife or his social position with the Atlanta black elite."

"Why didn't you ever tell me any of this?" Eric asked.

Curtis laughed and said, "For the same reason you didn't tell me, of course! I was partly embarrassed, partly didn't want anyone to tell me the truth about what was really happening."

The waiter arrived with the food, and for a few moments they ate in silence.

"I'm scared I'm falling for him," Eric said softly.

"You know how this will turn out, sweetie, right?"

Eric picked at his salad in silence.

"I don't want to see you get hurt. You deserve to be with someone who you can really be with. Someone you don't have to hide with."

"It just all happened so fast. The sex was…"

"Amazing," Curtis answered for him. "It's the taboo factor. It adds to the excitement. But trust me there's nothing like making love with someone who loves you completely, who doesn't treat you like you're something to be ashamed of. I'm glad every day that I met Tim."

Eric had always been slightly jealous of Curtis' relationship with his boyfriend. Sure, the two had had there ups and downs, but they truly were in love. Eric wondered if he'd ever have that. And sleeping with Marcus had started having him doubt if he even deserved it. It was sort of like the shame of the relationship, the fact that he couldn't seem to end it that made him think less of himself…and hopeless. Was sex alone enough to make him think he didn't deserve what Curtis had with his boyfriend?

"Is it truly making you happy?" Curtis asked.

Eric shook his head and said, "No. It isn't."

"I think you know what you need to do as difficult as it may be."

Eric nodded, but wondered deep down if he really had the strength to break things off with Marcus.

"I look hot in this, don't I?" Rochelle's friend, Carrie Anne, said as she spun around in the dressing room checking herself out from all angles while trying on a tiny little red dress in an upscale boutique in the chic Phipp's Plaza mall.

Carrie Anne's husband worked for Rochelle's father in the finance side of Sugar and Spice, and Rochelle found herself spending time with her…well, for lack of much else to do sometimes. Carrie Anne was an ex-Miss South Carolina. With her perfectly coiffed long blonde tresses, baby blue eyes, and perfectly proportioned tits and ass, she still very much looked like a beauty queen. She could also be exhausting with her obsession with…well, herself. But she always proved to be a diversion when Rochelle needed one.

The trouble was that Carrie Anne wasn't doing her goddamned job this time. All Rochelle could think about was Tyrone, the almost sex, and his running scared once her mother appeared. She couldn't remember the last time she had wanted a man inside her so badly.

She certainly hadn't felt that way about Marcus in a long time. Her mind also kept wandering to guessing what the PI would turn up on her husband. There had to be another woman. There just had to be. Problem was she wasn't certain how she would react once getting the news for real.

McNairs don't get divorced.

Her mother's words repeated over and over in her head like a damn CD stuck on the same musical chord.

Nope. If she wanted to stay in her family's good graces…but really, what did it matter? She found herself questioning it *all* finally. Was it really worth being in a loveless, passionless marriage? Just coming close to having sex with Tyrone had changed everything.

Tyrone.

She wanted him more than ever. If she could just get him alone again, she was sure she could get him to give her what she needed. But outside of him showing up to work on the pool or gardens, she didn't know how to contact him.

No.

She had to meet him somewhere else, somewhere her mother couldn't pop up.

"Hello?" Carrie Anne said, with her hands on her hips. "Where were you just now?"

Rochelle snapped back to the present, looked at Carrie Anne, and told her what she wanted to hear.

"You look stunning," Rochelle said.

"It does look great, doesn't it?" Carrie Anne squealed, admiring herself in the mirror.

Normally, some retail therapy did wonders for Rochelle but not today. She took a look around the boutique and remembered her dream in college while studying business about opening her own chain of upscale boutiques. Her father wasn't the only one in the family with a drive for business. But her parents had quickly squashed her idea when she approached them with it. Instead, they told her that the proper route was to become a society wife. *That* was her ultimate duty to her family. She knew what her father really meant.

Leave the business to the men.

It took all Tyrone had not to gasp when he walked into Nate Jenkins' office and saw Marlene Luclaire standing in front of a camera with a big smile on her face while Nate and his office staff sat at the same table as before.

Marlene *Fucking* Luclaire. The hottest black actress in Hollywood. Make that Academy Award winner for her role as an ex-lover of Malcolm X in the movie "The Revolution." She was even more gorgeous in person and had even been called America's African-

American princess by Ebony. With her rich dark skin, such the opposite of usual prized pale skin, long wild curly hair, almond shaped eyes, and standing at five feet ten inches tall, she was a gorgeous sight to behold.

And here she was looking at him and smiling.

"Tyrone Daniels," Nate Jenkins said. "This is…"

"I know exactly who this is," Tyrone let slip before he caught himself. Damn, he didn't want to look so starstruck, but he couldn't help it.

"How are you?" Marlene purred, smiling a fantastically beautiful gleaming white smile.

"I'm great," Tyrone said.

"I think you have a fan," Nate said, smiling.

"Sorry," Tyrone said, feeling a little embarrassed. "I didn't expect to meet you today."

"Marlene is playing the female lead in my new film, and she was gracious enough to come down to the ATL to do screen tests for us with potential actors. That includes you, Tyrone."

Tyrone felt Nate Jenkins' eye totally on him and not even looking in Marlene's direction. Nate appeared to be studying him closely and intently.

"Are you ready to make some screen magic with Ms. Luclaire?" Nate said.

"You bet," Tyrone said, hoping he'd remember the lines he'd been studying.

"Then let's shoot a test!" Nate said.

Walking back to his car, Tyrone could feel the butterflies in his stomach threaten to burst out. First, he got a call back for Nate Jenkins' newest movie. Then, he had the opportunity to actually screen test a scene with Marlene Luclaire, a romantic one at that! He never would have dreamed all of this possible just a few days ago.

If he had to say so himself, he knocked it out of the park. He even began to entertain the idea that he actually had a shot at this big break. Man, to think how much he could help out his grandmother if he got this role, it was almost overwhelming. He could finally buy her that little house in the suburbs with the white picket fence she had always wanted. He could change both of their lives forever.

He remembered he still needed to stop by another client's for a pool cleaning this afternoon. He'd almost forgotten in the excitement of it all. Maybe, just maybe, his pool cleaning days would soon be behind him.

He got into his truck and cranked it up. He could feel Nate Jenkins' gaze on him the whole screen test as if he were intently watching every move he made.

Yes!

He had a chance at this, and if he got it, he was going to make sure he didn't disappoint anyone!

Rochelle felt an overwhelming feeling of relief when she arrived home and found everyone gone, even the maid. Her thoughts and worries about what the PI might find out had been completely eclipsed by the idea of being fucked by Tyrone…and fucked well.

Her damn mother. Always screwing things up for her.

As she had watched Carrie Anne finish up her purchases, Rochelle realized that she had to go after Tyrone whatever it took. She believed with everything in her that he wanted her just as much as she wanted him. She just had to contact him outside of her parent's home.

She walked into her mother's office and surveyed the beyond organized space. There wasn't so much as a random paperclip or a stray piece of paper to be seen. But somewhere in that office there had to be Tyrone's phone number. I mean her mother had to collect that information, right?

The key would be to search for it without moving anything out of place to raise her mother's suspicions.

First, she looked over the desk without moving anything.

Where would her mother keep that kind of information?

She sat down in the leather chair next to the desk and began to carefully open each drawer. If the slightest thing were out of place, her mother would notice.

Imelda always noticed everything.

The first two drawers turned out just to be full of office supplies: pens, sticky notes, staples and the like.

When she opened the third drawer a wave of shock hit her when she discovered a small handgun at the bottom of the drawer.

"What the fuck?" she muttered to herself.

Her mother had never mentioned having a gun in the house. When did Imelda get the gun and why?

Rochelle had always hated the idea of having a gun in the house. They scared her, especially the thought of her ever having to use one. She didn't trust herself to use it correctly.

She gingerly moved the gun aside in the drawer and hit pay dirt when she found an address book. With two fingers, she carefully pulled out the address book and began to flip through its pages until she found the entry she was looking for.

Tyrone. Pool. 404-555-9873

She took out her own cell phone and programmed the number into it before putting the address book back to where she found it.

Finally.

She'd get her chance with Tyrone to get the kind of pounding she needed. *Then* she'd work on her marriage with Marcus. But she deserved a treat, and she couldn't think of a tastier one than Tyrone.

Before closing the drawer, she took one more look at the gun and shook her head. She obviously couldn't tell her mother she found it without giving away her snooping. But in an odd twist, she found herself admiring the handgun's gray steel sheen. So, much power in a small object. She felt fear and awe all at the same time.

Marcus just couldn't bring himself to head straight home right after work, so he walked down 14th Street and headed to the Four Seasons hotel under the pretense that he was meeting a new possible pastry vendor for Sugar and Spice. The harsh Southern humidity added to his sense of being oppressed, and he could feel the sweat dripping down his back underneath his dress shirt.

His feelings of his life closing in on him, threatening to suffocate what was left of a spark inside him were only increasing. Most days he was able to take out his frustration on Eric's hot little ass, but his father-in-law had managed to put the kibosh on it today with that lunch meeting, and he was growing worried that Eric appeared to be developing feelings for him that he couldn't return. He could see it in Eric's eyes when he penetrated him. The little white guy's look of pleasure mixed with devotion set off every warning signal in his mind.

Every day was becoming more and more of a struggle to get through. He found himself on some days wanting to physically tear his office apart...the office...*his cage*. He wished he could tell his in-laws to fuck off and tell Rochelle that no amount of nagging would ever get him to want to really be with her.

His ability to escape from the drudgery of his life had decreased more and more with each passing day. It had gotten to the point that he had found himself daydreaming about just running away, leaving his job behind, releasing himself from Rochelle's clutches. The daydreams had increased to the point that he actually found himself thinking out the steps from withdrawing all of the money from his bank account and buying a one way ticket to a Mexican resort town to...he didn't know for sure...open a bar, a shop. More than anything he yearned to start a new life. He knew it was unreasonable and only a pipe dream though. As miserable as he was, part of him thought he deserved it because he had let everyone, including himself, down by not being able to overcome these sexual feelings for men.

As he entered the busy lobby of the Four Seasons, he looked around for the bar. The only way he'd be able to face his wife and in-laws tonight would be to get highly buzzed first.

***

Dan Wells walked a good twenty yards behind his target, Marcus DuBois. The husband hadn't met up with the white guy from work today. He'd followed Marcus throughout the day from his arrival to work, to a lunch meeting, to now as it looked like DuBois was making a beeline for the Four Seasons. Maybe now he'd meet up with the same guy as the previous day.

Rochelle DuBois wanted an update soon. He was always a little curious to see how the spouses would react to what the evidence suggested. Some, despite hiring him, would remain in denial, some had a look of revenge enter their eyes, and some would break down in tears. A lot of the time, he could predict what each person's reaction would be even from the little bit of time he spent with them. But Rochelle DuBois was a hard call. If pressed, he'd have to guess she'd be either revenge focused or a crier.

Dan, carrying a briefcase to blend, waited a few beats before walking into the Four Seasons after Marcus DuBois. He saw DuBois head to the bar and order a drink.

Hmmm…was he waiting for another rendezvous with another man?

"Where's Marcus?" Rochelle asked her father, when she walked into the dining room where her parents were already seated and eating their dinner of prime rib and fresh steamed seasonal vegetables.

"I was wondering if you were coming down to dinner," her mother said, cocking an eyebrow.

Rochelle had been hoping they would be almost done and ready to move on to the study where her father would read the newspaper, still a paper edition, and her mother would watch C-SPAN. However, it looked like they had just sat down a few minutes before.

Rochelle ignored her mother and looked at her father for an answer regarding Marcus's whereabouts.

"Marcus was meeting a possible new vendor for drinks at the Four Seasons. He should be here soon."

Vendors? Hmmm. Rochelle wasn't convinced. But all she could obsess over at that moment was working up the nerve to call Tyrone and telling him point blank what she wanted from him.

"Maybe the two of you should plan a romantic getaway. Savannah is always a good choice," Imelda commented in her passive aggressive way.

Rochelle sat down and began to serve herself. She knew what Imelda was really suggesting and that was that she and Marcus should go somewhere and fuck like bunnies to make a grandkid.

"That would be nice. But someone keeps him busy at work," she replied, looking pointedly at her father and placing the blame on him.

"He has vacation time. He just needs to use it," her father said, bursting that balloon.

Whatever, Rochelle thought to herself. She'd deal with Marcus *after* getting what she needed from Tyrone and seeing what the PI uncovered for her.

Marcus sat the bar nursing a scotch and postponing the inevitable of having to head to his in-law's home.

"Another, sir?" the bartender asked, when his glass neared the empty point.

"Please," Marcus answered, pushing the glass towards the bartender who poured another for him.

Out of the corner of his eye he could see a table where a group of people were laughing, drinking, and looking like they were having one hell of a grand time. The group consisted of one woman and three men, all black, and there was something about the woman and one of the guys that looked familiar.

He sipped his drink, and he caught one of the guys glancing his way every few moments. The guy glimpsing at him was most definitely handsome, not in a muscular worked out way, but he had a combination of pretty boy looks mixed with an aura of intelligence.

Maybe it *was* time to move on from Eric. It would be a sticky situation, and he probably should have never started banging someone at work. But it would be better to end it now that let the guy get more attached. What he needed was someone just like him. Maybe married. Kids would be good, too, since it would make him more tied to his wife. He wanted a man who just wanted to fulfill his carnal urges like he did.

Holy. *Shit.*

He finally recognized the woman as Marlene Luclaire, only the hottest black actress around. A lot of movies and television shows had started shooting in Atlanta since it had a cheaper to produce "city" look than NYC or downtown Los Angeles. So, it shouldn't be a complete surprise that he'd see her at the Four Seasons.

Marcus tried to be discreet at stealing peeks at the group. But for a brief moment, his eyes locked with the guy he was sure had been checking him out. The guy then got up from the table and headed to the bathroom as the rest of the group continued what appeared to be a celebration.

Was he reading the gaze lock right? Was the guy giving him an invitation to follow him into the bathroom?

Marcus hesitated at first and wondered if he should risk it. Finally, the liquid courage from the alcohol convinced him that he should at least go check things out.

He stepped down from his chair at the bar and headed to the bathroom.

Dan Wells had been furiously typing on his laptop and nursing a beer to blend in with the crowd in the bar when he noticed DuBois making direct eye contact with a guy at a nearby table. He immediately recognized the woman at the table as at the actress Marleen Leclaire, and the man who had been looking at DuBois looked very familiar, too.

When the guy who had been checking DuBois out headed to the restroom, Dan could practically see the wheels turning in DuBois' head.

He's wondering if he should follow him, Dan thought. The two of them are very much cruising each other.

DuBois got up and headed to the bathroom.

Dan pretended to type out a text message and took pictures of him as he headed into the bathroom.

When Marcus walked into the bathroom he saw the guy from the table standing at a urinal. The guy looked at him and smiled while taking a step back to give Marcus a look at his long shaft. Marcus thought for a short guy he was pretty damn impressive with his huge dangling cock.

They continued to stare at each other as Marcus headed over to the urinal next to him.

Let's see how far he takes it, Marcus thought.

The two of them pissed in front of each other, hot streams of urine, pulsating out of their piss slits. At this point, neither of them played off the fact that they were checking each other…and their equipment out.

"Sup?" the guy asked, as he finished pissing but did not make an attempt to move.

"Hey," Marcus replied, finishing but not moving, too.

"Nice cock, dude," the guy said, his eyes fixated on Marcus's piece.

"You, too."

The guy started stroking his dick with one hand and rubbing his balls with his other. With his head, he motioned over to the one stall.

"Want to come check it out closer?" the guy asked him.

Marcus felt the adrenaline of a clandestine encounter pumping through his veins. The idea of exploring a new guy's cock mixed with the tabooness of the location was proving to be too tempting to resist.

"You want my cock?" Marcus boldly asked.

"Fuck yeah, man. But we gotta be quick," the guy responded.

Marcus nodded, and the guy went into the stall with Marcus behind him. Marcus locked the stall door, grateful that the door went all the way to the floor increasing the odds of privacy in case someone walked inside.

Marcus grabbed for the guy's penis and enjoyed feeling the engorged member in his hand. As much as he liked to fuck Eric, he wasn't hung like this guy, and he felt an erotic thrill wrapping his fingers around a man whose cock had a girth that rivaled his own. The heaviness of the guy's dick and bull balls was a huge turn on. Marcus had always been exclusively a top when it came to having sex with men. Somehow he could justify in his mind that he wasn't really totally gay because he was the one who did the fucking. But lately he had been fantasizing about what it must feel like to have another man penetrate him, and when it came to many things in life, Marcus thought you might as well go big or stay home. This guy undeniably *big*.

"You've got a nice piece," Marcus said, half-whispering in the guy's ear and stroking the guy.

Up and down. Up and down. Marcus used the guy's precum to help his hand glide back and forth over the entire length of the guy's dick.

"You, too, man," the guy replied in a husky voice.

Then before he knew it, the guy dropped to his knees and practically engulfed Marcus's entire cock. The guy fed hungrily and eagerly as if he were starving and Marcus's dick was dinner. The guy had an expert tongue that teased Marcus's dickhead in all the right places at all the right times. His mouth was hot and wet and sending Marcus into ecstasy.

"Fuck. Feels good," Marcus groaned, as he started to skullfuck the guy who appeared to have no gag reflex as Marcus's colossal piece of meat skull fucked the dude.

The guy took a quick break from nursing on Marcus's dick, looked up at Marcus and said, "I can't stay much longer, but I want you to come in my mouth. *Please.*"

Marcus just nodded and shoved his penis back into the guy's waiting mouth. In his mind, he thought about what it would be like to have this guy shove his own dick into his ass…a hard, rough, and unyielding kind of fuck. He bet this guy could screw him real good with that weighty mantool.

The thought of taking it up the ass from this guy sent Marcus straight to an orgasm as he started to come…hard…into the guy's mouth. The guy sucked down the spooge as if his life depended on it.

After Marcus had stopped coming and the guy stopped feeding, Marcus leaned back against the wall in the stall catching his breath.

The guy stood up, put his cock back into his pants, and looked at Marcus with continued lust in his eyes.

"I want a longer session with you," the guy said, licking his lips as if he had just finished a five star gourmet dinner.

"Okay," Marcus said. "How do I reach you?"

"I need to be discreet," the guy said, with a brief look of concern on his face.

Marcus held up his hand to show his wedding ring and said, "Like I don't?"

The guy nodded, reached into his back pocket, took out his wallet, and handed Marcus a card that had no name and just a phone number.

"Call me tomorrow," he said, placing the card in Marcus's palm and then quickly exiting the stall.

Marcus stood there for a moment still processing what had just happened…and how hot it had been. He heard the bathroom door open and slam shut and knew the guy had left the bathroom.

He looked down at the card that just had a phone number and the initials N.J. That's when it hit him. The guy had looked so familiar, and he had been with Marlene Leclaire. The dude was Nate Jenkins, the fucking movie director.

Holy.

Fuck.

He just got sucked off by an Oscar winner!

Marcus started to chuckle.

Maybe things were looking up after all…in more ways than one.

Dan Wells had counted the minutes DuBois was in the bathroom with the guy. Five minutes. The other guy, who he snapped a quick picture with his phone first, walked out first. About a minute later so did DuBois. Of course, these pictures didn't really prove anything, but they more than added to his suspicion.

Rochelle sat on the bed in her bedroom and stared at her phone. She'd been trying to work up the courage to call Tyrone for twenty minutes. It certainly wasn't that Tyrone had no idea that she was into him after their last encounter, but the sting of his running out still resonated with her. She told herself that had it not been for Imelda showing up she would have gotten exactly what she needed. He was just spooked by her mother. Imelda did that to people anyway.

She glanced at the clock and saw that it was after eight. She walked to the window and looked downstairs to make sure Marcus's car wasn't parked.

Nope. Still not home. But what was unusual about that?

While still staring out the window…just in case…she dialed the number she had found for Tyrone. She could feel her heart rate accelerate as she hit each number on the touchscreen phone. When the phone began to ring, she wondered for a moment if this was the right thing. What kind of fire was she playing with actually?

The problem was she knew what she wanted to play with. It wasn't fire, but it was definitely hot.

"Hello?" she heard Tyrone answer.

For a moment, she lost her voice. She didn't know how to the point she should be. Should she make up some excuse about needing to talk about his work at the house? Or should she just go right ahead and tell him she wanted what she was sure was a weighty piece of manhood shoved inside her until she wanted to scream in absolute divine pleasure.

"Tyrone, it's Rochelle DuBois," she finally said.

There was a second of silence before Tyrone said, "Uh, hello, Ms. DuBois."

"I just wanted to tell you I'm sorry about what happened in the pool house."

Sorry that you did get to fuck my brains out, she thought.

"Uh, don't worry about that. It'll stay between us. I was out of line."

"That's the problem, Tyrone," she said. "You were totally *in line*, and I can't stop thinking about it. I want to see you tomorrow."

"I'm not sure that's a good idea since I work for your parents," he said with each word sounding like a very deliberate choice.

"This has nothing to do with my parents, Tyrone, or the work you do here. But I really do need to see you to...talk. Please, give me just a few minutes of your time."

She hated that she used the word *please*. She was Rochelle McNair DuBois, and as hot as Tyrone was, he was still in a different social class. Yet, here she was begging for a few more private moments with him. She despised that he had this control over her. But if she were truly going to try and reset her marriage with Marcus, she'd be damned if she didn't get some fun in beforehand especially if he'd been hooking up with other women.

"Okay. I could meet you in the late afternoon," he finally said.

"At your place?" she asked, knowing her voice betrayed her by revealing her hopes.

"I'll text you the address. What about five tomorrow?"

Five. That would be pretty late, but she'd tell Marcus she had a dinner planned with some friends from college that were in town. He wouldn't question it.

"Five would be great," Rochelle said, already feeling wet down below at just the thought.

She saw Marcus's Mercedes coupe pull up in the driveway.

Just in time.

"See you tomorrow, Tyrone," she said, her voice purring as she ended the call.

Tyrone stretched out on the full sized bed in his tiny studio apartment. He knew that having Rochelle DuBois over to his place could be nothing but a bad idea. But he was a man, and he *had* been thinking about what would have happened between them if her mother hadn't popped up right before things got even more heated. He would have fucked her good. Maybe in the afternoon he'd give her what she obviously wanted.

He wished his dick didn't have a mind of its own sometimes and let him make questionable decisions such as this. But maybe he would need the job at her parents' house much longer. Between work, auditions, and checking in on his grandmother he hadn't had much time to fulfill his sexual desires.

He looked around his cramped apartment with the futon that had seen better days, dirty dishes in the sink, and clothes strewn around everywhere. He'd have to straighten up a bit before she got here in the afternoon. Although, he doubted she'd care too much. He knew what she wanted, and she'd probably wouldn't care about the state of his apartment but just the *size* of his cock.

He was still on a high from his audition and testing opposite Marlene Leclaire. If someone would have told him a week ago that he'd get a call back on a Nate Jenkins film, he would have thought them crazy.

His phone buzzed again, and he wondered if it might be Rochelle again wanting to change the time...or maybe head over now.

When he recognized the number as the same one that had called him from Nate Jenkins' office he practically jumped up in bed. He took a deep breath and answered.

"Hello?"

"Tyrone? This is Nate Jenkins."

Shit. It was the director himself.

"Uh...hi," Tyrone stammered.

"I was wondering if you'd be open to meeting tomorrow and discussing more about the role and my vision for the movie to see if we might have a fit for you and a role."

"Yeah! Yeah, of course!" Tyrone exclaimed.

"Great."

"What time should I come by your office?"

There was a slight pause before Nate Jenkins said, "Actually, I thought it would be good for you to stop by my house in a much more relaxed environment. After all, if I end up working with someone for a few months I want to get to know them some *outside* of the office."

Nate Jenkins' house! Tyrone was blown away.

"Of course," Tyrone said. "That'd be no problem at all."

"Excellent. I'll have my secretary call you in the morning with the address and some more details. See you tomorrow, Tyrone."

"Thanks," Tyrone replied still not believing his luck.

It just all seemed just too good to be true.

"How was your day?" Marcus asked, as he took off his work clothes and changed into jeans and a polo shirt.

"Good. And you?"

"I'm great," Marcus said. "What happened with you today?"

Rochelle noticed that her husband seemed in a much better mood than he'd been in quite a while. He had a glow about him that she couldn't remember seeing in a very long time. She wondered if that glow had to do with another woman.

Well, whatever happened next, whatever she found out from the PI, she would use that as a starting point to rebuild their marriage.

"Just some work on the hospital charity ball. It was good. I'll be having dinner with some old college friends that are on the board for the charity tomorrow if that's okay," she said, changing into a simple floral print dress for dinner.

"Of course," Tyrone said. "Have fun."

Oh, I plan to do so," Rochelle thought.

"Dinner smelled great when I walked by the dining room."

"Cook made Father's favorites," Rochelle replied.

Even having dinner with his in-laws wasn't enough to dampen his good mood after the hot encounter he had with the film director. He left the business card with the phone number in his car. If the bathroom encounter had proven to be so hot he could just imagine what a longer…more private…session could be like.

She felt better than good, she wanted to say. She wanted to tell him that she was planning on getting the deep dicking she needed tomorrow. And after that, he was going to have to end whatever he was doing on the side. If they were going to inherit the Sugar and Spice empire, they were going to have to become a united front once again like after they first were married. Marcus had been so focused back then with every part of their life, including their marriage. Rochelle had never allowed herself to fail and this marriage would not be the first thing…no matter what she had to do about it.

"I've been thinking," she said, as she slipped on some saddles.

"About?" Tyrone asked, cocking an eyebrow.

She knew she was using what he had coined as her "all business voice."

"I think it may have been a mistake to stay here with my parents throughout the whole remodel. Mother and Father have been very…gracious, but I miss our privacy. If it's going to take more than a month longer, maybe we should look at renting a corporate apartment."

She noticed that a wave of relief spread across Marcus's face.

"You mean it?" he asked. "I've thought about bringing it up, but I didn't want to upset you."

"It seemed like a good, easy solution at the time," Rochelle said, walking towards Marcus and tentatively putting her body just mere inches from his. "But I think we'd both be happier in our own place."

She wrapped her arms around him, and for once, he didn't seem to stiffen…in a bad way…in response. She tipped her head up and placed a kiss on his, and he responded back with a teasing of his tongue between her lips.

She didn't know if this rare moment of affection had to do with her body pressed against his or his utter relief at moving out of her parent's house.

Chapter Five

Dan made a notation in his phone when he saw the young guy from Marcus DuBois office enter the hotel lobby at 12:15 in the afternoon. He casually stayed a few steps behind him, but followed the guy into the elevator.

As the elevator ascended to the twenty-first floor, Dan checked the guy out from out of the corner of his eye. Dan had always only been into pussy, and, well, tits and ass. He'd never messed around with another guy before, but he'd be lying if he said he hadn't at least thought about it out of curiosity once or twice...not that he'd go there. Still, if you were going to fuck a dude, this young guy would probably be a good pick. Dan noticed how the guy was definitely more pretty than say handsome. He had slightly delicate features, big blue eyes, a trim body, and a bubble butt that you could probably bounce a quarter off of.

The young guy didn't notice Dan checking him out at all. In fact, he looked to be a million miles away in thought. So, when the elevator opened and Dan followed him out, the guy didn't even appear to notice.

"Hello?" Dan said, pretending to answer his cellphone but instead taking a picture of the guy going into Room 2115.

Dan kept walking as the guy went into the hotel room and shut the door behind him.

Now he'd wait for Marcus DuBois to show up. And just like clockwork, Marcus emerged from the elevator, and Dan started walking towards him and once again pretended to be talking into his phone.

"I'll be home tomorrow night," Dan said into the phone while discreetly also taking a picture of Marcus DuBois going into the same hotel room.

Dan knew he had what he needed to give the wife an idea of what was going on. To find out her husband was probably fucking the gay guy from the office was going to be a blow. Dan had seen it before. Wives figure they can fight for their husbands…if they want…against another woman. But another man? How can you even compete with that?

This afternoon he'd get his answer on how exactly Rochelle DuBois would take the news.

"I can't do this anymore," Eric said, as soon as Marcus walked through the door of the hotel room and started to loosen his tie.

Marcus froze and cocked his head. He looked as if he couldn't comprehend what Eric had just said.

Usually, they would have been tearing off each other's clothes within the first few seconds with little to no words exchanged. Eric would be preparing himself mentally for the wide and deep penetration that would come from Marcus. And Marcus would speak to him in a rough, hurried, lustful voice with kinky phrases of desire.

Instead, Eric sat in the chair at the room's desk fully clothed with a solemn look on his face and the beginning of tears in his eyes.

"What do you mean?" Marcus demanded.

"Exactly what I said, Marcus" Eric said, getting up and walking towards him. "I've given this a lot of thought. This is just a road to…"

"Road to what?" Marcus said, anger in his voice.

Eric got up and walked towards the large window and looked down at the traffic on the downtown street.

He couldn't look at Marcus while he said this. If he did, his resolve might weaken.

"I'm starting to feel things for you, Marcus," Eric said softly.

Marcus walked over to him and got close enough that Eric could smell the faint smell of Marcus's aftershave.

"We talked about this, Eric, when started all this. That it would just be sex, no emotions, just…"

"That's easy for you to say, Marcus. You're the one that's the closet case!" Eric exclaimed.

Marcus took a step back and stayed silent. He looked completely thrown.

"Not me!" Eric continued. "I want more, and I can admit that now. Continuing this affair is going to get me nowhere near what I need and *deserve*. I see my friends with their boyfriends and…"

"You knew I couldn't give you that," Marcus said. "But are you really willing to give up what I do give you?"

Marcus never saw this coming. Sure, he was already thinking it was time to end things with Eric, but he always thought it would be on *his* terms. Now that Eric was the one cutting it off, Marcus immediately felt anger at being the one who was blindsided. He had always pictured himself as the one who was ultimately in control of this situation. Eric's ass was his when he wanted it. Or so he thought. This is what he got for getting involved with a guy who was out and wanted to explore…feelings.

"What you give me is not enough," Eric told him. "I want someone to come home to, someone I don't have to sneak around with and meet in hotels."

"Whatever then," Marcus said, tightening his tie. His head was spinning at the loss of control over this situation, this affair. "You don't want this anymore," he said, grabbing his crotch through his pants to show off the bulge Eric had worshipped over the past months. "Then you won't get it anymore."

"Marcus, I just can't…" Eric started to say.

Marcus held up a hand, turned around, and walked out of the room.

As he headed towards the elevator, he remembered the business card from Nate Jenkins in his car. *That* was the type of man he needed, one who would understand what he required in a mutually beneficial relationship, and what he wasn't willing to give up just so people would know he liked to fuck guys in their asses. He shouldn't have even messed around with a little twink like Eric to begin with.

Rochelle was sitting in the salon chair at Weavin' Wild getting her extensions, imported from India, tightened when her phone vibrated in her purse. She wanted to look her best when she met up with Tyrone for what she hoped would be the best fuck she'd had in years.

Her stylist, Billy Wilson, a thirty-ish white guy with long blonde hair, who was ironically the hottest hair stylist for black women in Atlanta with the two month waiting period for an appointment to prove it, rolled his eyes as the phone went off. She knew he hated it when his clients tried to talk on their phones while he worked.

When she saw the call was from Dan Wells she couldn't wait to answer it.

"Sorry, Billy. My uncle is in the hospital," she lied. "You mind if we take a five minute break."

"Five minute piss and snack break for me. That's it!" Billy said, "Mister Billy is on a tight schedule!"

When Billy was out of earshot, Rochelle answered her phone.

"Yes?"

"Ms. DuBois, I have the information I think you're looking for," the PI said to her.

"Good," she said, feeling both relieved that she would finally know what…or who…Marcus had been up to and terrified to find out the truth.   After all, once she knew the truth there could be no more denying it.

"I'm going to say this once again, Ms. DuBois. Sometimes people only think they want to know the truth. It's not too late for you to just forget all this and…"

"No, I *must* know. When can I meet you?"

"Two hours at the location we met before. Is that good?"

"See you then," Rochelle said, before hitting the red touch button to end the call.

"Finished with your call, my queen?" Billy said, with more than a drop of sarcasm when he walked back over to her.

"I am. Sorry about that. Now finish making me beautiful."

"Do you know who this is?" Marcus said into the phone, as he leaned back in his office chair.

"The hot guy I got off with in the bathroom last night," the voice on the other end said.

Marcus felt his cock stiffen in his gray dress pants. He was still processing being the one to be dumped, and he needed the jolt some words of admiration gave him.

"Bingo," he replied.

"I was wondering if you'd call," Nate said.

"Let's say you made an impression."

"I aim to please."

"I could tell."

"I need to ask you something."

"Yeah?"

"Do you know who I am?"

"Yeah, I know. I figured it out afterwards," Marcus answered in a hushed voice, watching his co-workers walk by his door. He knew he should be hammering out another marketing report for his father-in-law, but the thought of that boredom couldn't complete with the thought of another hot encounter…especially after Eric ended things between them. He wasn't sure how he'd be able to face Eric at work, but he only had himself to blame.

"Then you probably know I need to be…"

"Very discreet," Marcus answered. "I'm in the same situation."

"Good. Cause I don't fuck around with my reputation…or anything that might affect the future box office performance of my films. I've worked too hard to get to where I am."

"Me, too," Marcus replied.

"Good. Come by at six, why don't you? I'll have a surprise for you later. One that I think you'll really enjoy."

"And what would that be?" Marcus asked, feeling his stomach knot up when Eric, who stared straight ahead, walked by his door.

"Wouldn't be a surprise if I told you, right? I'll text you the address. See ya then."

And with that Nate Jenkins hung up the phone.

"Priscilla?" Marcus called out to his new secretary, a twenty-three year old just out of college and eager to please.

Priscilla quickly popped into his office carrying a legal pad.

"Yes, Mr. DuBois?" she asked.

"Cancel my four o'clock meeting," he said.

"Yes, Mr. DuBois. What should I tell *them* is the reason?"

Them would be his father-in-law when it got down to it.

"Tell *them* I have food poisoning, and I had to leave."

"Anything else, sir?" Priscilla asked.

"That's it. Thanks."

"Yes, sir," Priscilla said, quickly leaving.

Yes, a guy like Nate Jenkins was exactly the kind of *friend* he needed.

Traffic moved faster than expected, so Rochelle arrived earlier than she thought to that horrible run-down neighborhood she had first met the PI.

Thank God for tinted windows, she thought. At least none of the nefarious looking characters that stumbled down the street could stare into the car and see her.

She'd been replaying in her head the phone conversation with the PI over and over. She realized that deep down there was still a part of her that hoped he would uncover nothing even as unlikely as that seemed. Now, she felt even more determined to have her fuckfest with Tyrone.

It was her due.

She checked the time on her watch and saw it was three o'clock. Taking a deep breath to steady herself, she hopped out of the car, locked it, and made a beeline for the dive bar. A few of the street people stared at her curiously as she hightailed it to the bar's door. She knew she stood out like a cheap whore at a Paris couture fashion show here, but that was also what made it safe in a way. The likelihood of running into anyone she knew here was pretty much zero.

When she walked into the bar, she was automatically hit by the overpowering scent of some sort of bleach based cleaning fluid and the smell of fried foods.

Only a few hardcore drunks sat at the bar slouched over mugs of cheap beer.

Disgusting.

Dan Wells sat at the same booth when she met up with him before. He greeted her with a slight nod of the head as she slid into the booth seat opposite him.

"Something to drink?" he asked.

"I'm fine," she said, tightlipped. "Just tell me what I need to know."

"I have pictures," he said, picking up a manila envelope that lay on that seat next to him. "Would you like to see?"

"Well, I'm certainly not here for a prayer meeting," Rochelle snapped, her nerves more edge than ever.

"I just have to ask," Dan said, opening the envelope. He took out the pictures and spread them across the table for her to see. "While tailing your husband I discovered that he spent lunch hours at this nearby hotel. You can see him here entering the lobby on two separate dates. Here's one of him heading into the hotel room."

Rochelle studied the pictures closely, but she didn't see him with a woman in any of them.

"Who's he meeting?" she demanded.

"This guy," Dan said, laying out the pictures of Eric at the same hotel, going into the same room.

"What?" Rochelle asked confused. She recognized the young guy as Eric, an assistant from her father's office.

"Do you know this guy?" Dan asked, pointing at a picture of Eric entering the hotel room.

She nodded and said, "From Marcus's office. So, what are you saying?"

"Ms. DuBois, after following your husband that past few days, I'm pretty sure he's been having an affair with this young man. I also have pictures of him having what I think was a sexual encounter in a bathroom at the Four Seasons with another man."

Rochelle sat in stunned silence for a moment trying to process all of this. She finally said, "You're saying my husband is having an affair, but it's with a man?"

"I'm pretty sure of it, yes."

"Are you serious?" Rochelle asked, chuckling.

This had to be a joke or some sort of mistake that could be explained away, she thought.

"I'm very serious. I'm sorry," Dan said, stone faced and without a hint of a sorrowful tone in his voice. Instead, he sounded like an automated computer voice devoid of emotion.

"An affair with a man? With Eric?"

Rochelle began to feel slightly nauseous.

"I can continue to follow him if you'd like," Dan said. "But I think we'll just find out more of the same. Of course, extra pictures and information might help you in a divorce proceeding especially if I can get a picture of them in a *physical* situation."

"My husband's gay?" Rochelle mumbled.

Her mind was spinning now as she thought back over the years of passionless sex and long hours supposedly at the office.

"Well, I'd say he's at least bisexual. Not that it probably makes you feel any better, but this is hardly the first case I've done with this outcome."

"Are these mine?" Rochelle said, staring at the pictures.

"Of course," Dan said. "I can make additional ones if you need them, too."

"That's fine for now," Rochelle said, pulling herself and her demeanor together.

I am not going to lose my shit in this rundown dive bar, she thought to herself.

"I'll contact you if I need anything else," she said, businesslike.

She gathered up the pictures and quickly exited the bar.

Fuck. She needed a drink, but it certainly wasn't going to be here.

When she made it back inside the car, she let out a blood curdling scream.

That fucker!

How dare he humiliate her like this. Fucking around with another woman would have been bad enough, but he had made a total fool out of her. Her whole marriage, all of these years when she was in the prime of her life had been wasted away on a man who could never give her what she wanted. Oh, but he sure took what he needed including a plum spot in her father's company. She'd been used as a pawn in a closet case's game of secrets and lies.

She could kill him with her bare hands right then and there. How she'd love to choke the life of him and to see suffering in his face.

She thought of Eric from his office. Marcus even had the nerve to fuck some little white guy who worked for him. They probably made fun of her, mocked her, talked about what an idiot she was. And she just knew there were people at that office who knew what was going on. They probably talked about her in their break room and discussed how clueless she must be. That little white fairy probably joked about it with his friends. How dare Eric have the nerve to work in her father's company and have her *husband* fuck him!

She took a deep breath to try and steady herself and took out her phone and dialed the Sugar and Spice corporate headquarters.

"Sugar and Spice. How may I direct your call?" the receptionist asked.

"Give me Janet in HR," Rochelle demanded.

"May I ask who's..."

"This is Rochelle McNair DuBois. Give me Janet in HR *now!*"

"Certainly," the receptionist replied.

After a few rings, Janet, who'd been working for her father for over twenty years answered the phone.

"Rochelle. How nice to hear from you," Janet said a little too cheerfully.

The receptionist must have let her know that Rochelle sounded in a mood.

"Hello, Janet," Rochelle said, doing her best to sound friendly. "I was wondering if I could ask you for a favor."

"Certainly," Janet replied in a voice that said she was anything but certain about it.

"That assistant, Eric, in my father's office. Do you know him?" Rochelle asked.

"Yes, I do."

"Well, he went far and beyond what would be his usual duties."

Like fucking my husband, she wanted to say.

"He really helped out Marcus with some matters that needed attention, and it just made the biggest difference."

"That's wonderful to hear. Eric's a hard worker," Janet said.

Amongst other things, Rochelle thought.

"I wanted to send him a thank you. Maybe some chocolates or one of those fruit baskets."

"That sounds very nice," Janet said carefully, obviously wondering how she fit in with all of this.

"I wanted to send it to his home instead of the office. You know how office gossip can be, and if he gets a present from the boss' daughter, well, I just wanted to be more discreet with it."

"Um, okay. Would you like for me to have him call you with his address?"

"I'd rather it be a surprise," Rochelle said. "Could you give me his home address?"

"Well, that goes against policy. You know privacy laws and such and…"

"Please, Janet. Just for me. I really want this to be a nice surprise for him."

"Well…" Janet said. "I suppose I could…"

"Excellent!" Rochelle said, before Janet could figure out a way to get out of it. "Please email the address to me. I believe you have my email."

"Uh, yes. I think I do."

"I'll expect it this afternoon. Thanks, Janet," Rochelle said, ending the call.

Rochelle wasn't sure exactly what she would do to make Eric pay yet for being part of her husband's plan to humiliate her, but she'd make sure he got his due just as much as Marcus would get his.

She remembered that her time to meet up with Tyrone was coming up fast, but her hands were shaking from a mixture of anger and hurt. She saw a liquor store a block away. She hated to get out of the car in this type of neighborhood again, but that's what she needed. Just a few shots of something strong to erase this nightmare out of her mind for a bit. She needed Tyrone to make her feel like a woman again...to give her what her husband obviously couldn't. Then she'd decide how to proceed...and how to make both Marcus and Eric pay for what they had done to her.

Chapter Six

Tyrone had just gotten off the phone with his grandmother sharing the good news of his second callback for the Nate Jenkins movie when there was a knock at his door.

Shit.

Rochelle DuBois.

He'd almost forgotten that he had agreed that she could come over for an obvious booty call. He hadn't even had a chance to pick out what to wear to Nate Jenkins. As much as he would normally be all into a woman like Rochelle, he had bigger more important fish to fry besides just getting laid. The truth was he really didn't have time for her at all with everything he had to do. He wished he would have remembered to call her and cancel or at least postpone.

When he answered the door he found Rochelle leaning against the doorway with an obvious glassy eyed expression on her face. Girl was loaded.

"Hey there, baby," she cooed while practically stumbling into his apartment.

She threw her arms around him, and he had to hold her up so she didn't fall.

I hope she didn't drive here, he thought.

"Rochelle, uh, hi. Looks like someone already started the party," Tyrone said, gently leading her to his futon for her to sit.

"It's been a day, *baaaabbbyy*," she slurred. "I really need a man like you to get me through it."

She started pawing at his crotch and pants zipper.

Falling down drunk had never been a turn on for Tyrone, and this situation was no exception.

"How'd you get here?" he asked, still standing up and guiding her hands away from between her legs which just seemed to agitate her more. She looked sloppy and desperate…a very unsexy combination. "You didn't drive, did you?"

She just shrugged her shoulders and stared up at him.

"Make love to me, baby. Make me feel good," she begged.

Her eyeliner was smudged and her usually perfectly coiffed hair was in disarray with random strands sticking out in all directions.

"I think maybe you need some coffee right now before anything. Let me go make you some," Tyrone said, gently pushing her hands away.

Rochelle, stumbling, pulled herself up.

"I don't want any fucking coffee!" she exclaimed. "I want some dick. And you're giving it to me if you know what's good for you!"

He didn't like the threatening tone in her voice either. He certainly didn't need this shit. If putting her off lost him the McNair job, then so be it. Dealing with the mess that was Rochelle wasn't worth it.

"Let me fix you some coffee and call you a cab. I don't think sex is what you need right now," he said.

"What the hell are you saying? Are you really turning me down? After you invited me over here?"

She slumped back down onto the futon and sank into the plush cushioning.

He wanted to remind her that she had basically invited herself over, but he decided that wouldn't be the right approach.

"I think you just need to sleep this off. Look, I'm going to go fix you some coffee and call you a cab. I think you need to go home."

He headed into the kitchen to look up a cab company on his phone and make her a cup of instant coffee…*to go*.

"You know, what?" she yelled from the living room. "Fuck you! Fuck all men! I was going to be the lay of your life. Ain't none of y'all real men. Not a one!"

Tyrone cursed at himself for agreeing to this to begin with. He wished he would have known what a hot mess she was earlier. This was the last shit he needed before his meeting with Nate Jenkins.

He ordered a cab and boiled some water.

"Just lay down until the cab gets here. Things will be better tomorrow," he said in what he hoped would be a calming voice.

But when he walked back into his living room, she was gone. The door to his apartment was wide open. He went outside and looked down both sides of the street. He couldn't imagine where she'd gone in that condition, but he decided he couldn't be worried about it. He needed to go back in and get ready for what he hoped would be a life-changing meeting.

"I was wondering if you'd really show up," Nate Jenkins said when he opened his door.

Marcus had thought his in-laws lived in a garish McMansion, but their house had nothing on this one. Nate's house had to be at least twice as large with elaborate gardens of numerous flowers and a koi pond out front. Parked outside in the circular drive was a red Porsche convertible, Marcus's dream car. It looked as if Nate Jenkins had already made a lot of his dreams come true.

Marcus had heard rumors that Nate might be gay. He was never seen with a date besides his mother at awards celebrations, but he was also careful never to appear with a man in a situation that could be questionable.

Marcus envied all the man had already managed to accomplish. Success and all on his own. Nate wasn't tied down to a wife and demanding in-laws like he was.

"I'm a man of my word. If I say I'm going to be here, I'm going to be here."

"Come in. I gave the staff the night off. We're the only ones here," Nate said, motioning for him to come inside.

When Marcus walked in he found a house that was decorated in ultramodern, sleek furniture with a lot of it the finest leather. The walls were adorned by abstract art that looked like something a kindergartener might paint but that Marcus was sure must cost a hefty price.

"What's your name by the way?" Nate said, closing the door.

"Marcus."

"Well, Marcus," Nate said, walking towards him...closer and closer...until they could smell each other's manliness. "I'm glad you came by."

And then without another word, Nate dropped to his knees, unzipped Marcus's pants, took out his dick and began engulfing Marcus's weighty dark manmeat once again.

Dude was a cocksucking master!

"Holy fuck!" Marcus managed to croak out as Nate masterfully sucked his full length...up and down...up and down...tongue swirling around his dickhead, teasing his piss slit.

"You like that?" Nate said, breaking only momentarily.

"Fuck, yeah," Marcus said, as Nate went back to work with expert cocksucking skills.

Within a couple of minutes, Marcus couldn't hold it anymore. He started shooting his piping hot, salty load right down Nate's throat.

Nate greedily sucked and swallowed down every last drop.

Marcus felt breathless with his head spinning. He hadn't meant to come that fast, but he'd never, *ever*, been on the receiving end of cocksucking skills of that caliber. Eric was a pro, but Nate obviously had his doctorate in Dicksucking Theory.

"Sorry, I came so fast. I usually..."

Nate, with a smile on his face, stood back up and simply petted Marcus's dick like it was a pet snake.

"Don't worry about it. My cock sucking usually takes guys by surprise the first time. Besides..." he leaned in until his mouth was mere inches from Marcus's, "I enjoyed every last drop, and I'm sure you have another load in you."

He put Marcus's dick back inside his pants and zipped him up.

"Come in and have a drink," he said, taking Marcus's arm and leading him into the living room. "What's your pleasure?"

"Uh..." Marcus said, his mind still reeling from what had just happened. "A beer."

"A man after my own heart. Beer it is! Have a seat," Nate said, motioning to the couch. "I'll be back in a moment. Oh, and I have a surprise later."

"A surprise?" Marcus said curiously.

"Yep," Nate said, heading into the kitchen. "And I think you're going to love *him*."

She wasn't sure how she made it home, but somehow she had. Her mind was still cloudy and confused about everything that had happened during the day. First, finding out that her own husband was a queer and then being turned down by the pool boy. Who the fuck did these men think they were screwing with her life?

She swung open the front door to her parent's house and was met with silence. No parents, no staff, no sissy cheating husband. *Nobody*. She suddenly had a vague memory of her parents telling her they had a charity ball to go to for the evening. As for Marcus, he was probably off fucking that little white guy.

She kicked off her heels right there in the hallway and stumbled down the massive hallway leading to the center of the house.

"Goddamn fuckers," she spat.

She'd been made a fool of…first with her entire marriage and then by a damn blue collar worker. Not to mention that little queen at her father's office who probably laughed behind her back and spread vicious rumors. All these years doing what her parents expected her to do…college, marriage, be the society wife. No one ever asked what *she* wanted to do. No one cared. They just all used her. Even her parents used her when they trotted her out to be shown off to their society friends as the example of what the perfect daughter should be.

She made her way into her mother's office where she knew a bottle of sherry sat on top of a bar. Might as well down that while she was on a roll, she thought.

But when she walked into the office another thought hit her. *The gun.* That little beauty of a pistol her mother kept in one of the drawers. Wow. The power that piece of medal would give her. That'd be one hell of a way to get their attention…all of them! And she knew just who to start with.

Nate and Tyrone spent a good hour heavily making out, grabbing each other's dicks and asses, pawing each other like animals in heat with only a day left to breed. It was raw and intense in a way that Marcus hadn't had with Eric. It was as if the secrets that ruled both of their lives made this sexual encounter even hotter…two souls in sync with the needs of the other both physically and the need for discretion.

Just when Tyrone thought they were moving towards actual fucking…and as surprised as Tyrone found the thought, he wondered what it would be like to have Nate Jenkins, an Oscar winner, pound his ass….make him the bitch for a change…the doorbell rang.

A big smile spread across Nate's face and he said, "The surprise is here."

"You still haven't said what kind of surprise," Tyrone said.

"Just follow my lead. Go along with what I say. Understand?" Nate said, making his way to the foyer. He turned one last time and looked back at Marcus and repeated, "Follow the lead. Okay? It'll be fun."

"Okay," Marcus said, his curiosity piquing.

"And you might want to zip your pants," Nate said, before disappearing.

"Hi. Come in," Marcus heard Nate say from the foyer.

"Thanks," a deep husky voice answered.

Nate walked back in with the hottest piece of eye candy Marcus had seen in a long time. This brother wasn't just good looking. He was fucking beautiful. And he looked oddly…familiar. But Marcus couldn't place it, but he knew he'd seen that face before at some point.

"Marcus, I'd like you to meet Tyrone. He's been auditioning for one of the most important parts…the Jessie one," Nate said. "This is Marcus. He's one of the executive producers of the film."

Okay, now I'm officially confused, Marcus thought. But Nate shot him a look to remind him to play along.

"It's a pleasure to meet you, man," Tyrone said, walking up to Nate and shaking his hand.

"Likewise," Marcus said, looking back at Nate and wondering where the hell this was going.

"We had Nate screen test with Marlene. So, I thought it'd be good to have him come over and talk with us about the part. Maybe…" Nate looked at Tyrone. "Maybe you can read another one of the scenes for us."

"Sure. I'd love to!" Tyrone exclaimed.

"Great!" Nate said. "I really need actors who are…*open minded* when it comes to my creative process."

Eric couldn't believe he'd let Curtis talk him into a blind date. But Curtis had been after him for weeks to meet a guy from his office.

"He's cute, smart, and most importantly not married to a woman," Curtis had cracked on the phone earlier in the day.

Finally, Eric had relented and agreed to meet the guy for coffee…at a Sugar and Spice, of all damn places, in Midtown in a couple of hours.

Even though he had plenty of time to get ready, he was already obsessing about what to wear. It had been so long since he had gone on an actual real date he wasn't even sure how to go about it.

Part of his heart still stung at the thought of Marcus. Even though deep down that there wasn't a chance…he had still hung on to the false hope that Marcus might proclaim his love and his separation from his wife.

What an idiot you've been, he thought. So much wasted time and hurt feelings.

Just when he had put on a pair of CK jeans and a Ralph Lauren polo and was examining the effect in the bathroom mirror, he heard a knock on the door.

He had no clue who that could be. Jehovah's Witnesses? No one ever stopped by without calling.

He decided to ignore it at first thinking it may just be a salesperson, but the knocking got louder and louder.

Finally, he made his way to the living room and called out, "Coming! Chill out, okay?"

When he opened the door he couldn't quite believe his eyes to see Rochelle DuBois standing there.

"Uh, Ms. Du Bois. Hi. What can I do for you?"

And then it just took one look in her eyes, and he immediately knew that she *knew*.

"I think we're past you being able to do anything for me, Eric. Since you've already been busy fucking my husband," she said, practically spitting out the words in madness. She then reached into her purse and pulled out just the top of a pistol. "Guess what? I'm going to talk, and you're going to do *a lot* of listening."

Chapter Seven

Tyrone sat across from Nate and this Marcus guy, who looked a little familiar, as the three made some small talk. Actually, Nate did most of the talking while this producer just sat there on the couch and nodded. Something just felt *off*. But Tyrone couldn't quite put his finger on it yet.

"How long have you been taking acting classes?" Nate asked.

"Three years now. I did some acting in some local play productions and a little print work with modeling."

"Well, you certainly have the model look," Nate said, his eyes fixated on Tyrone.

"Thanks," Tyrone said, feeling more and more uneasy under the gaze of these two men. "I'd love to hear more about the film."

"Yes, well, as you probably know many of my films cater to the underserved black female audience. They tend to focus on empowerment for these women, and well, the intended audience loves them and eats them up. Sometimes..." Nate's voice drifted off for a second. "I wish I could explore some other issues, but women..." he motioned to all the furnishings in the room. "Have been very good to me. So, who am I to disappoint? I don't like to disappoint. What about you, Tyrone?"

"Uh, no. I'm a hard worker," Tyrone answered.

"I'm sure you are," Nate replied. "And tonight I need you to show me just how much of one you are."

Marcus started to find this whole situation more than odd. This guy was the *surprise*. If he was here for sex, he appeared to have no clue, and this whole role play with him being a "producer" was even more unnerving. What the fuck was going on here?

"Marcus was very impressed with your screen test, weren't you, Marcus?" Nate said, suddenly turning and looking at him expectedly.

"Uh…" Marcus stammered. "Yes."

He hoped that was the right answer.

"See, Tyrone. You've wowed us all which is why I've had you come over here tonight.   My audience in addition to the women empowerment themes, well, they like to have their Prince Charming, their fantasy stud in the movie.   After all, if I'm creating a woman's fantasy, there has to be the handsome charming man.   That's where the Jessie role comes in."

Marcus watched Nate reach for a manila envelope that Marcus hadn't noticed before now. He picked it up and reached out to give it to Tyrone.

"I'd like you to read and act out this scene for us if you don't mind. And while you do so, I need you to keep in mind the audience we're looking to serve. Could you do that, Tyrone?"

Tyrone tentatively took the envelope from Nate. Marcus could see a look of slight confusion in the guy's eyes, and Marcus realized that whatever "surprise" Nate had in store for the evening this young guy wasn't clued in…at all.

"Go ahead," Nate urged. "Take out the pages. I have to warn you that the scenes are of a somewhat sexual nature. This is why it's just us here tonight. I wanted you to feel comfortable going through the scene the first time. But I also need to be able to see that you can do it…that you can act out scenes of this nature and also convey the scene's truth."

Tyrone watched the guy nod his head but stay silent.

"If you'd like, I can give you a few minutes to prepare. Marcus and I can go into the kitchen to rustle up some snacks while you get into the space you need mentally. Is that good?"

"Uh, sure," the young guy said.

"Excellent," Nate said. "We'll be back in just a few moments."

"Ms. DuBois, I don't know what you think…" Eric started to say.

"I speak first, you little fucker," Rochelle said, after she charged her way inside and drove Eric into a corner of the living room. She held the pistol not pointed at him but at the floor. But she kept it visible at all times. This little queen was going to know she meant business. She reached with her free hand into her purse and pulled out a bottle of scotch which she managed to unscrew with one hand. "You liked making a fool of me, didn't you?"

"Look. Really. I don't know what you're talking about," Eric said, holding his hands up in protest.

A flash of anger went across Rochelle's face, and, suddenly, she was now pointing the gun straight at him.

"Don't speak to me like I'm an idiot!" she screamed.

"I'm sorry! I just…"

"I hired a PI. I know all about your little regular hotel rendezvouses with my husband. Did you like sucking his dick?"

Tears forming in his eyes and shaking from fear, Eric couldn't gather himself enough to answer.

"Did you?!" Rochelle demanded.

"It was a mistake. All of it. I'm so sorry. It's over. It really is. I swear!"

"Oh, you swear, huh?" Rochelle said, unsteadily taking a step towards him.

Eric noticed now just how intoxicated she really was.

Shit. Was this how it would all go down and end? Would his desire for taboo dick…for not believing that he deserved better lead him to his own *death*?

"Do you have any idea how humiliated I feel?" Rochelle asked. "Do you?"

"I…uh…" Eric stammered.

The truth was he tried *not* to think about her. When Marcus was on top of him and inside him, he liked to pretend that he was the only one that Marcus penetrated…that he was the "wife." But now with her standing there shaking with a gun in her hand, he couldn't escape what he'd been doing the past few months and how those actions impacted more than just himself.

"And what about HIV?" Rochelle spat. "If my husband has been *fucking* men, how do I know he hasn't infected me? Jesus, just the thought that I may have to take pills the rest of my life because my son-of-a-bitch careless husband…"

"We were always safe! I swear!" Eric exclaimed, his hands shaking.

"You'll excuse me if I don't take your goddamn word for it. And how do you know what he's done with other men? Huh? Answer me!"

"I…I don't know," Eric admitted. He didn't like to think he may have been one man of many.

"My whole entire life…it's been no more than a lie," Rochelle said, inching closer and closer to him with the gun by her side. Her eyes started to well up in tears. "I guess no man could ever really want me."

"That's not true," Eric replied in what he hoped was a calm voice. He had to talk her down and get the gun from her.

"It is true," she said, her voice dripping with bitterness.

She stumbled and sat on the couch while her body swayed slowly back and forth.

Eric thought his heart would beat right through his chest. He'd never been this scared in his whole life and without an idea of what he should do.

"No man has ever wanted me. No one has ever wanted me," she mumbled more to herself than Eric.

Eric slowly began to ease along the wall towards the bedroom. He needed to just get in there, lock the door, and call the police.

"You're a beautiful woman. I'm sure many men would want you," Eric said, keeping his voice even.

"How would you know?" Rochelle demanded. "How would you know anything about my life? My mess of a fucking life!"

She looked down at the gun in her hands and a look of disbelief came over her face. He thought she looked like someone who just woke up to find herself in a bad dream. She looked at him and then back at the gun.

"Ms. DuBois?" Eric said in a quiet voice. "Please...you don't have to..."

Then she started to sob. The pistol dropped out of her hand and hit the floor, and she buried her face in her hands as she started to cry uncontrollably.

Feeling like this was the moment, he dropped to his knees, crawled over, and slowly picked up the gun and moved back from her.

She looked up at him, and the anger was gone. All he saw was sadness, disappointment, and desperation, and Eric felt waves of guilt that he actually helped drive someone to this point.

"None of it has meant anything," she said in a half-whisper.

"I'm sorry. I really am," Eric said, backing up further away and keeping the gun close to him.

But what to do now?

Rochelle, suddenly looking near sober, surprised him when she suddenly stood up and said, "It doesn't matter anymore. I know that now."

And with that, she walked out of his front door without looking back.

Eric sat the gun on the floor and quickly went to the door and locked in behind her.

"Holy shit," he muttered, sweat pouring off his forehead.

Eric couldn't believe all of that just happened in a matter of minutes. The woman had a gun pointed at him! His first thought was to call the police, but he immediately thought of the scandal that would break out once word got out that Rochelle DuBois' husband had been fucking him! But if he didn't do anything, what else might she do?

Instead, he went to his bedroom, grabbed his phone, and dialed the person who had to know what just happened.

"What the fuck is going on in there?" Marcus demanded, once he was in the kitchen with Nate.

"Just chill, man. We're going to fun. Trust me. He's smoking hot, right?" Nate said, taking out some wine glasses and setting them on the marble counter.

Marcus felt his phone vibrate in his pocket. He took it out and saw it was Eric's number. The last thing he needed was some sort of change of mind plea from Eric. He probably had thought it over and decided that he didn't want to break it off after all. What else could he be calling for?

Drama queen.

Marcus hit the "ignore" button his phone and looked back up at Nate.

"Look, that guy think's he here for an audition or something…not whatever fooling around you have him for. He looks uncomfortable."

Nate poured the wine and shook his head as if Marcus were a naïve child.

"He's an actor," Nate explained in a condescending tone. "You'd be surprised what they'll do for a part…whether their gay or straight."

"Man, this is fucked up," Marcus said, shaking his hand. "I don't feel comfortable doing this if this guy…"

And then it hit Marcus. He knew he'd seen the actor guy before. He'd briefly met him one day at the McNair house. He was their pool guy slash gardener.

Oh. Shit.

"Look, man," Marcus began, his nerves shot to hell now. The last thing he needed was this guy connecting him to Rochelle. "I can't do this. Whatever kink you have in mind…forcing this guy…"

"Forcing!" Nate exclaimed. "No one is forcing anyone to do anything. But you'd be surprised what people will do to make their dreams come true."

"Dude, this is messed up. It's one thing for us to mess around.."

"Don't fucking get high and mighty with me, man. You're the one that's married and fucking around with dudes behind your wife's back."

First, the affair with Eric. Now this. He thought maybe this could be the easy side thing he needed to keep himself going. But what kind of person was he becoming especially if he went ahead with this guy's plan to pressure the actor…who may or may not recognize him… into having some sort of *quid pro quo* sex. Everything, after years of circumventing two worlds, was suddenly and quickly spiraling out of control and making him feel like a piece of shit.

"I can't do this," Marcus said. "I'm sorry. I'm leaving now."

"Whatever, man. Fine. But if you can't handle it, don't bother to call."

"I won't," Marcus said, turning around and leaving the kitchen.

Tyrone couldn't believe the pages he was reading. The supposed "scene" involved him stripping off *all* of his clothes, touching himself all over, and then telling the "actress" in the scene how he was going to make love to her, and there was no holding back in the dialogue. There was no way this scene was for a real movie that was rated anything but

X. It certainly wasn't something that Nate Jenkins would ever film for one of his fucking chick flicks for a mass audience.

That's when Tyrone realized that this whole thing was anything but an audition. Nate Jenkins didn't want him for a part in a movie. He just wanted to humiliate him and act out some sort of kink fantasy. He was being used. It had all been nothing but a ruse to get him here and to somehow take advantage of him.

Tyrone felt embarrassed, used, and mocked.

Suddenly, the guy who was supposed to be the producer entered the living room again but this time speed walking like his pants were on fire.

"Hey! What the hell is this about?" Tyrone demanded.

But the producer guy just breezed by him without making eye contact.

I know I've seen him before, Tyrone thought. He was more sure now than ever.

"I'm talking to you, dude!" Tyrone yelled after him.

But the guy went into the foyer and then out the door. Tyrone heard the front door slam.

"He had an emergency," Nate Jenkins voiced said behind him.

Tyrone turned around and saw the director standing there with two glasses of wine.

"What's really going on here?" Tyrone demanded.

"What are you talking about?" Nate said, shrugging his shoulders. "We're here to talk about the movie and you having a possible part in it?"

Tyrone chuckled bitterly.

"There's no way these pages would be in a movie you'd do," Tyrone said, pointing to the scattered pages on the glass coffee table. "You think I'm some sort of idiot?"

"Whoa!" Nate exclaimed, placing the glasses of wine on a side table. "Watch your tone, dude! Who do you think..."

"You brought me over here for some sort of…some sort of…" Tyrone couldn't bring himself to say it.   He didn't want to admit that he'd be taken advantage of like this.

"I brought you over here to *audition*," Nate emphasized.   "But obviously you're not open to what you need to do for a role. You need to think about that, Tyrone. Breaks don't come easily, and a part in my movie could change your life."

Nate started to walk towards Tyrone, who balled his hands into fists at his sides.

"Now I ask you. Would doing me a little favor that only the two of us would know about be that big of a deal?"

Suddenly, Nate was standing just mere inches from Tyrone.   He stood so close that Tyrone could smell his cologne, a sweet scent which made him vaguely nauseous now.

Tyrone looked down, and he could make out the outline of Nate's hard-on through his linen pants.

Fuck.

He was right. This was all one big set up.

"So, what are you going to do, Tyrone? You know what they say? A hole's a hole. Would it really be that different for you to fuck me in the ass? Like you've never done that to a woman before…a strong, black man like yourself."

Nate walked an inch closer, and before Tyrone knew it, Nate placed his hand in his crotch and started grabbing for his dick.

"Whoa, man! Back the fuck off!" Tyrone yelled. "Touch me again, and I swear to God I'll fucking break your skull!"

Nate quickly stepped back and said, "Fuck you, man! Like you didn't know this was what's up! You really think you're that great of an actor? That you're special? There's at least ten other men who'd do what's needed for a part in my film."

"I would never fucking whore myself out like that!" Tyrone yelled back.

Nate laughed mean spiritedly.

"Then you need to rethink an acting career and get real," Nate spat.

"Fuck you! I'm outta here!" Tyrone exclaimed heading towards the foyer.

"Hold it!" Nate demanded.

Tyrone turned around for a brief second, and he saw how Nate's eyes had narrowed.

"You mention a word of this to anyone, and I'll make sure you never even get work as a fucking extra! You understand?" Nate said, a slight fear of panic showing on his face.

"You think I'd ever mention this fucked upness and the fact that I got taken to anyone?"

"You better not if you know what's good for you," Nate warned.

"Fuck. You," Tyrone replied heading towards the door.

"No! Fuck you, man!" Nate screamed after him.

Tyrone practically ran out the front door letting the door slam behind him.

Once Tyrone was sitting in his truck again, he took deep breaths to slow his breathing.

What would he tell his grandmother when she asked how the audition went?

Had he been stupid to think that he ever could make it as an actor in the first place?

He caught a glimpse of himself in the rearview mirror and studied the reflection. He always been told he was a "looker" but was he more than that? Could he ever be more than that?

As Marcus walked up the stairs of his in-law's house, he thanked God that they were nowhere to be seen. After the day he had, he didn't know if he could deal with them. He didn't know how he'd face Rochelle. Between seeing the screwed up situation with Eric and then with the movie director, Marcus knew this…whatever his life was…couldn't continue this way. But he didn't know how to get out. His entire life had become being the husband of Rochelle DuBois, the heiress of a fucking coffee house chain. His job was a far cry from the business he'd always imagined starting on his own.

When he reached the top of the stairs, he saw the light was on in the bedroom he shared with Rochelle. He'd just jump in the shower and hope she'd let him crash.

His phone vibrated again. He pulled it out and saw that he'd actually missed nine calls from Eric.

He couldn't deal with him right now, and he didn't know how he'd deal with it when he saw him tomorrow at the office.

When Marcus opened the bedroom door, he found Rochelle sitting on the edge of the bed. He could tell she was crying and her mascara had run down her face. The dark chocolate brown tresses that framed her face looked frizzed and frayed.

Marcus paused before walking in further. He didn't know what the fuck was going on now, but taking one look at the usually composed Rochelle, he knew something major had gone down.

What the hell had happened now?

"Rochelle?" Marcus asked cautiously. "What's going on?"

She looked at him with dead eyes and motioned to a suitcase on the floor.

"You're leaving tonight," she said her voice oddly void of emotion.

"Wait? What are you talking about?" Marcus asked.

He noticed pictures laying spread out across the bed. He walked in closer to take a look, and he froze. There on the bed were pictures of him and Eric going in and out of their hotel room.

"What's this?" Marcus croaked.

"Pictures of you. Pictures of your male *lover*. I hired a PI. Finally, after all of these years of listening to pathetic excuses for why you weren't ever at home, I wised up, Marcus. I decided to take control of the situation. Now I know. And now you're leaving and going far, far away from here."

"Rochelle, I don't know what you think…"

"Shut up!" Rochelle screamed. "Just shut up, Marcus! I'm done being used by you."

"I didn't use you. You were the one who pushed this marriage," Marcus countered, even though he knew the excuse sounded weak.

Rochelle started to laugh a manic laugh that Marcus had never heard from her before.

"This is all a misunderstanding," Marcus said meekly.

He already knew though that it was over. It had all caught up with him. In some respects, he had expected this day. One day she'll find out or she'll catch me, he'd thought over the years. He'd be exposed, and the career he'd sacrificed so much for would be over.

"You'll leave before my parents get back tonight," Rochelle continued, her voice void of emotion. "I have no desire for *anyone* especially them to know what kind of man you are."

Tyrone bristled at the words "kind of man."

"I *will not* be humiliated any more than I already have been," Rochelle said. "I'll tell my parents that we split because we were both unhappy. They'll freak the fuck out at the thought of a divorce in the family, but they'll have to get over it. You'll leave your position at Sugar and Spice. I'll make sure my father gives you a generous severance.

This will be in exchange for you keeping your mouth *shut* about the real reason."

Defeated, Marcus said, "Secrets have a way of coming out one way or the other."

"This one better not. *Ever*. No one can know what you did to me, you sorry bastard."

Marcus nodded. He knew he had no choice. He'd seen the wrath of Rochelle before when supposed friends wronged her. She'd destroy them with her venomous tongue. She'd make sure he'd never get a decent job again, and he was smart to know he'd brought much of this on himself. It was true that he'd used her to move up the social and corporate ladder to leave his days of his lower middle class upbringing behind him.

She glanced at the suitcase and said, "I've pack enough for a few days for you. I'll send you what I think you *deserve* at a later date. Understand?"

"Yes," Marcus croaked.

"And one more thing, if I test HIV positive…"

"I was always safe!" Marcus declared, realizing she had no reason to believe him even if it was true.

"Excuse me if I'd rather get a test to tell me that. But if you also infected me, I swear to God I will make every one of your last days a living hell."

Marcus *had* always been safe and made it a priority. Thank God! Because he didn't doubt what Rochelle said to him one bit.

"Rochelle, I'm so…"

"Take the suitcase and go!" Rochelle barked, averting her eyes, refusing to look at him.

Marcus knew he'd been defeated. Without another word, he picked up the suitcase and walked out of the bedroom heading towards a new and completely unknown life.

Epilogue- One Year Later

As he sat outside at a Midtown café waiting for his boyfriend, Lucas, Eric thought back and couldn't believe it had been a year since that night Rochelle DuBois came to his apartment with a gun. To avoid a scandal he didn't want to be a part of, he never called the police. Marcus never returned any of his calls that night, and Eric was shocked to find out the next day at work that Marcus and Rochelle were divorcing and Marcus quit Sugar and Spice with no notice.

He had immediately gotten rid of the gun by driving out to Lake Lanier and tossing it into the water. Eric didn't want to be connected to anything from that horrible night, and that also meant his job at Sugar and Spice. He made a few calls that week to some contacts and ended up getting a similar job in marketing for a grocery store chain.

Lucas, with the romantic gestures and warm personality, had been the guy he was supposed to meet the night Rochelle had shown up. Shaking and upset, he had composed himself enough to call and reschedule. He'd never expected to fall in love though...and with a man who was out and emotionally available. For the first time, Eric had decided to take a risk, open his heart, and see what could happen.

"Hey, handsome," he heard Lucas say behind him and felt his boyfriend's strong hand on his shoulder.

Eric turned around and looked up to see Lucas standing there with a bouquet of spring flowers.

"Happy anniversary!" Lucas said, bending down to give Eric a kiss.

Rochelle rearranged some of the jade and turquoise jewelry items in the storefront window of the boutique, Blasé, she owned in a historical building in the Peachtree area. After Marcus left, she sold the house they were remodeling for a tidy sum, cashed out some of her trust fund, bought a condo downtown and opened the business *she* had always dreamed of owning. For once, there was something that was completely hers and not wrapped around her parents or a man.

Her friends, including Carrie Anne, were perplexed why she'd want to take on the work of owning a shop instead of just simply shopping. But she'd never been happier going into work almost every day and being an active owner and manager of her boutique.

Men…

Well, she'd gone on a few dates here and there, but the sting of Marcus's betrayal and her willingness to ignore it for so long proved to be too fresh in her mind.

One thing she knew for certain that if there ever was another man she'd have him thoroughly checked out even going as far as hiring a PI to follow him until she was satisfied. She'd never be victim of a cheating man…and a man on the down low again.

With his grandmother's encouragement, Tyrone decided not to let the night at Nate Jenkins' house destroy his dreams. He took his meager savings and moved to Los Angeles to really pursue acting. After months of waiting tables and working as a bouncer at various bars, he landed a small part in an underwear ad campaign and suddenly found himself on billboards around the city. Before he knew it, he was cast in a supporting role in an action film, *The Right Way*, starring one of the biggest African-American actors in Hollywood, Devon Holland, a former soap actor who made it big when he got cast as in a police detective series.

Tyrone suddenly find himself on the fast track…moving so fast in fact, it sometimes felt like he had to run to keep up.

On the first night of shooting, Tyrone was in heaven on the set mixing and networking with the other actors, many of which he'd seen on TV and in movies. But when he heard a distant but familiar voice walking towards the set he froze. He turned around to find Devon Holland and Nate Jenkins walking towards him.

"Tyrone, man, I want you to meet an old friend of mine, Nate Jenkins. He's going to be our new….and better director for this film," Devon said.

Tate's arm was wrapped around Nate's shoulder, and Nate had a huge shit eating grin on his face.

"Hello, Tyrone. We meet again," Nate said, with a smirk.

Tyrone felt a wave of nausea sweep over him.

No. Fucking. Way.

Marcus thought he'd be prepared for New York summers. After all, he had survived the humidity in the South his entire life. But New York being the concrete jungle that it was, proved to take the summer heat to a new level. Despite the weather, he wouldn't trade his time in New York for anything. It had been a very hard road, but life had truly began to blossom in new ways he thought he'd never experience…or that he didn't deserve to experience.

As he sat in the New and Out and Proud support group at a local gay and lesbian community center, he once again listened to stories that often weren't that different from his own. Most men who came out at his age had had similar experiences…wives and clandestine meetings that left them feeling ashamed and full of self-loathing.

He'd headed to New York with no real plan once his promised severance came in from Sugar and Spice. He didn't contest anything about the divorce and ended up leaving most items from his life behind. After spending a few months slowly beginning the coming out process

by joining the support group and becoming involved in the gay
community, he slowly began to feel like he was discovering his authentic
self. *Finally.*

A friend he made in the support group also referred him to the HR
department at a marketing firm in Manhattan. And right before the
severance money ran out, he started a new job, a job free of the double-
life stress he lived at Sugar and Spice.

As the New and Out and Proud meeting started to wind down a
little, a first timer to the group, who Marcus had immediately noticed
due to his muscular dark good looks when he walked in, spoke and said,
"I don't know what to do. I don't know how to do this."

The guy, who was also black, had a husky but athletic build. His
black hair was in tight corn rows, and he wore baggy shorts, the kind
that could be pulled down in one quick motion, and a white t-shirt that
was tight in all the right places.

The guy had the same look of fear and confusion that Marcus knew
he must have on his face when he first arrived in town.

"Please tell us more. We're all here to help. No judgment," Rich,
the group's moderator said.

"My name is Stefan, and I've been living my entire life on the DL.
And…I can't do it anymore."

Marcus felt this immediate connection and attraction to this guy like
he had never had with anyone else before. It was as if he got struck by a
lightning bolt the moment Stefan walked into the room. Marcus wanted
so badly to reach out and touch him, hold his hand, and tell him it
would eventually be all okay even if the road to get there would be
rough.

"Hi, Stefan," Rich said, smiling warmly.

Marcus locked eyes with Stefan for a second, and he smiled at him
hoping to help put him at ease.

"I've never talked about this before," Stefan said. "My life on the down low has been...unbelievable and fucked up at times."

"We're here to listen," Rich replied. "Would you like to tell us more?"

Marcus watched Stefan struggle to find the courage to say the words that composed his story. Finally, Stefan said, "My story is a little crazy. *Sometimes* fucking hot. But I can't do it anymore. I have to get this off my chest."

Marcus scooted forward a little in his chair. He wanted to hear this man's story. He knew there were probably some similarities to his own story...just like most people in the group. But something told him there was something about this man's story that was going to be a little different...

About the Author

For more on Shondra Jackson, please visit www.chancespress.com. You may email Shondra at shondra@chancespress.com.

www.ingramcontent.com/pod-product-compliance
Lightning Source LLC
Chambersburg PA
CBHW071331130626
46556CB00004B/1843